CAMEL RIDER

PRUE MASON

 Charlesbridge

To Samantha, Sharon, Jan, Joan, Veronica, and Vaitsa of the Dubai Writers' Group, who were there when I wanted to give up; to Joyati, Surendar, Rooa, and the present staff of *Young Times* for making writing fun; and most of all to my husband and best friend, Kerry, who always believed in me and supported me, and to my second best friend, Tara, our dog.—P. M.

2009 First paperback edition
2007 First U.S. edition
Text copyright © 2004 by Prue Mason
Jacket design by David Altheim, copyright © 2004 by Penguin Group
    (Australia). Jacket photographs courtesy of Steven Wilkes and Philip Lee
    Harvey/Getty Images

Published by Charlesbridge, 85 Main Street, Watertown, MA 02472
(617) 926-0329 • www.charlesbridge.com

First published by Penguin Group (Australia), a division of Pearson Australia
Group Pty Ltd, 2004

Library of Congress Cataloging-in-Publication Data
Mason, Prue.
    Camel rider / Prue Mason.—1st U.S. ed.
        p. cm.
        Summary: Two expatriates living in a Middle Eastern country, twelve-year-
old Adam from Australia and Walid from Bangladesh, must rely on one
another when war breaks out and they find themselves in the desert, both trying
to reach the same city with no water, little food, and no common language.
    ISBN 978-1-58089-314-5 (reinforced for library use)
    ISBN 978-1-58089-315-2 (softcover)
[1. Survival—Fiction. 2. Deserts—Fiction. 3. Australians—Persian Gulf
Region—Fiction. 4. Bangladeshis—Persian Gulf Region—Fiction. 5.
Communication—Fiction. 6. War—Fiction. 7. Persian Gulf Region—Fiction.]
I. Title.
PZ7.M42313Cam 2007
[Fic]—dc22   2006034125

Printed in the United States of America
(hc) 10 9 8 7 6 5 4 3 2 1
(sc) 10 9 8 7 6 5 4 3 2 1

Printed and bound by Lake Book Manufacturing, Inc.

INTRODUCTION

Abudai is a fictional city, although it's typical of any one of the many oil-rich states in the Arabian Gulf. Before the discovery of oil in the area, the people lived in tribal groups ruled by sheikhs. They mainly lived in small settlements around central forts that were built near water, either the sea or an oasis. These people were fishermen, traders, merchants, pearl divers, date palm farmers and goatherds. There were also the Bedu, the nomadic people who lived in small extended family groups and who moved camps on a regular basis to allow their animals to graze on the sparse vegetation of the desert lands.

Because there weren't any lines on a map to show

borders between countries, there were often fights over territory between the neighboring tribes.

With the extreme heat, barren land, and lack of any modern technology, life was tough. However, the people of the Arabian Gulf endured their hardships and even thanked Allah for His blessings. Their way of life had not changed for hundreds of years.

Then in the 1960s when oil was discovered, progress, as we call it, was rapid. The mud-brick houses were pulled down and new concrete villas were built, and the Bedu began to move into towns where life was not so hard.

Now, where camels had roamed, there are busy airports carrying thousands of people to and from cities that have been built in less than fifty years. To build and run these modern cities, the local people needed skilled workers from many other countries, and people of many other nationalities and cultures came to live in the Gulf region. Most expatriates are from India, Pakistan and other Arabic countries; westerners make up only a small minority.

Because of past bad experience, the older generation of locals is often wary of foreigners, no matter where they come from. They still remember what it was like before the oil industry changed their lives, and they try to instill a sense of tradition in the young people. But as life becomes easier, living by the old ways seems more difficult.

Camel racing is one part of the old way of living that has survived the change—it is a traditional sport, although using young children to ride the camels is a recent development.

It should be noted that people of this area refer to the region as the Arabian Gulf, rather than the Persian Gulf, and that the Arabic words and phrases are spelled in a way that suggests how they sound in that region.

I love you, my brother, whoever you are—whether you worship in your church, kneel in your temple, or pray in your mosque. You and I are children of one faith, for the diverse paths of religion are fingers of the loving hand of one Supreme Being, a hand extended to all, offering completeness of spirit to all, eager to receive all.

Kahlil Gibran
The Words of the Master

PROLOGUE

A camel grumbles and mutters as it kneels on the ground. It has been hobbled, its back feet tied together, to stop it straying far from the camp where the small tribe of Bedu have set up for the night.

Around a fire, men sit cross-legged and talk, the dust of their journey washed from their faces and beards. A woman, dark as a shadow, slips out from underneath the draped coverings that make up their home for the evening. She is carrying a smoke black, heavy iron pot with a long, curved pourer. She fills little cups with aromatic but bitter coffee and hands one to each man. As they sip, some men look deep into the glowing embers of the fire; others chat about the day's journey and what may lie ahead on the long trip through the desert to the next oasis. One looks at the sky and sees a map in the darkness, pinpricked by thousands upon thousands of bright stars. From stories that have been passed down through generations, this man, like the others, can read the map and make his way safely through the ocean of red sand.

And the ocean is vast. For all he can see in any direction around him is the blackness of the desert, flat and stretching away to the horizon. As the stars move in a slow, wheeling circle in the darkness above, this man is aware of how small and insignificant he is amongst all this vastness.

Yet he is not afraid, because he knows exactly where he is. A point, unique to himself alone, that is directly above him becomes the highest point in the sky. He names it the "zenith." Then he imagines a straight line passing through his body and plunging deep into the earth to reach the lowest point, exactly below where he is sitting. This point he calls the "nadir."

As he looks into the glowing embers of the dying fire he smiles, for he knows he is at the center of the universe.

PART ONE WAR

CHAPTER ONE ADAM

MIDNIGHT IN ABUDAI, DAY ONE

I should be sleeping, but I'm all tense and nervous. Not scared-nervous. I should be, though, because Mum says she rang and told Dad what I did. He's going to kill me when he gets back tomorrow night. But I'll worry about that then.

I can't sleep. I just lie in bed and listen. All I want to hear is that heavy front door pulled shut. That'll mean Mum's really left and gone back to Australia without me and I'll be in the house, alone, for a whole day, until Dad gets home. Yes!

Well, of course, there'll be Chandra, but she's our

maid and she's always so busy downstairs cleaning and cooking.

I'm tingly-excited nervous because I can hardly believe my mind-bustingly brilliant brain wave has worked so well.

I can hear Mum moving around downstairs. She's ready to leave, but as usual is giving Chandra last-minute orders. Mum says that Chandra is very honest and reliable, but that her English is not good so she needs to be told things slowly.

Tonight Mum's so het up she's forgotten what she's always telling me and she gabbles at Chandra.

"Adam's father is due back from his flight at eleven tomorrow night," she says quickly. "He'll deal with Adam then, and no matter what that boy says he is NOT to be allowed out of the compound after what he's done. Oh, except to pick up his new school uniform. I meant to get it today, but with everything happening, I forgot. But he's got to come straight back here afterward. Now, is there anything else? Oh, that's right, there's a list of emergency numbers by the phone, and you know if anything happens to the dog the vet's number is there as well." She finally pauses for breath.

I hear Chandra saying, "Yes madam, yes madam," but I know there's no way she really does know what Mum is saying. For sure, though, she'll be shaking her head in that way that means yes, but looks like no.

Sarah, my older sister—who used to be really funny when we first came here—cracked me up when she took Chandra off, saying "Yes madam, yes madam," sounding just like Chandra does. But I was only seven when my dad got a job as a pilot for Abudai Airlines, and we left our home in Melbourne to live here in the Middle East. Sarah was thirteen then, and everybody said she was a brilliant actress. She's given up that idea now and turned all serious and boring. She says she wants to be a journalist instead.

It's funny, though, how quickly we got used to different things, like the way the Indians and Sri Lankans do all that head shaking. It just seems normal now. Like living in a compound is normal.

My mum still doesn't think it's normal to be living so close to other people who work for the airline. Dad says she should consider herself lucky. If she was an Arab woman, she'd be living in a compound with all Dad's relations. But I wouldn't mind living with Barby—that's my grandmother. And it'd be fun to live with some of my cousins. I guess the downside would be that there'd be more people to tell you off when you did something wrong. Plus, there's not much privacy. With all the houses being built around a garden in the middle, everyone can look through your windows and see what you're up to. Mum says it's like being inside a fishbowl. And then there's all the kids running in and out. That's the part I like, because all my friends live in the compound as well, and we can take turns to hang out at each other's places depending on whose dad—or maybe, if we're lucky—whose mum is away on a trip.

My dad reckons that in the future everyone in the world will be living in compounds like ours anyway, with high walls and guards at the gate. He says it will be the only way people will feel safe. I think that'd be brilliant. I love living in a compound.

I hear Mum rattling on again. "Of course, if you need anything, just go across the compound to Margot madam and she'll sort it out—I could kill that boy! But I have to go tonight to get there in time for Sarah's . . ." She doesn't bother finishing the sentence, and I can hear her footsteps hurrying up the stairs. Is she coming up to my room?

I begin to breathe deeply and evenly. If she comes in, she'll think I'm asleep. Even though it's midnight, and the car's waiting outside to take her to the airport, I wouldn't put it past her to drag me out of bed and give me another good telling off. She's pretty angry with me because I'm meant to be starting at my new school next Monday. Now I can't.

And she hasn't stopped going on and on about how Sarah's been looking forward to having her little brother back in Australia. As if! She probably just wants to convert me to her latest cause. Dad says we should give her a soapbox for Christmas. I just wish she wouldn't go on and on. Especially when she comes back here for holidays and starts going off about the way things are so superficial over here and how people are so materialistic and stuff. She's always going on about greedy expats and everything she thinks is wrong with modern life here—how it's all about the oil. It's embarrassing.

She used to be fun. When we were younger she could always think up brilliant games. And because she's such a good actress she could take anyone off. For a big sister she was pretty cool, because she even took the blame when we got into trouble, but that was before she went to boarding school and became superior and serious about stuff.

And just because I'm nearly thirteen now, Mum and Dad say I have to go back to Australia and go to boarding school there. They reckon it will give me roots. Like I'm a potted plant or something.

The thing is, they don't understand. I'm different from Sarah. I've got my friends. She missed her friends when she came over here, and she wanted to go back and be a boarder so she could have midnight feasts and pillow fights and all that girls' stuff. But I know what it's like. I know you can't go surfing in a boarding school, so I don't want to go.

My door opens.

"I love you, darling," my mum whispers. But I

keep my eyes tightly closed. It could be a trap. If I let her know I'm awake, I bet she'll go on and on again about how I should be ashamed of myself and how selfish I am and how I don't think of anyone but myself.

I just happen to think it was the ultimate, mind-bustingly brilliant brain wave to slip my passport into dad's flight bag before he went off on a four-day trip. It means that now I can't leave Abudai tonight.

I know I'll get a good blast from my dad when he gets back tomorrow night, and he'll probably make me get on the very next flight out of here, but it was still worth it. At least now I've got one more day of freedom.

CHAPTER TWO WALID
PREDAWN IN A CAMEL CAMP ON THE OUTSKIRTS OF ABUDAI, DAY ONE

"Mama! Do not leave me. I am so frightened. Mama!"

She kicks me. It's then I wake and look up at the face not of my mama, but of Old Goat.

He is like the devil with his scraggled beard, streaked with the henna he rubs through it to make it orange like a flame.

I am lying on the ground where always I sleep, and he kicks me again. I think it is from kicking boys that he is always limping, but he is saying that a camel stood on him when he held it at the start of the races. If only I had seen this. How I would have laughed!

I sniff the morning air. It is sharp and sour, full of the

odors of the night, of piss and tears. From nearby camps there are the shouts and curses of others as they, too, wake to this new day. Not far from me, underneath a shelter made from dried palm fronds, I see Badir and Mustapha. These boys are smaller than me, and like rats.

Old Goat hisses at me. "*Aiee,* Walid, boy! Be stopping that screeching like one *bint*—just like a girl, you are! Maybe, instead of *Walid,* we will be calling you *Bint.*" He cackles.

Once I had another name. But only in my dreams now am I remembering my life in my home country. In that time, back in Bangladesh, before I came to this camp to be a *rakeeba,* a camel rider, my mama said I was *Emir Saheer,* little prince. Now I answer to *Walid,* which means only "boy."

With quickness, I jump to my feet to stop Old Goat from kicking me once more. As all of my senses return to this world, I see I have been sleeping too long. There is grey light in the sky and all must soon be rising to say prayers—to thank Allah for making the night be over and ask for blessings of the day ahead.

Mostly I awaken first, for it is my duty to fetch water and boil it to make Old Goat's chai. He likes to have tea before his morning prayers.

There was once one other boy, Yasub, who made the chai. He was bigger than me, but he is gone now. He is dead. He told me that Old Goat has been living in this camp for many many years and that he is older than sin, so he cannot die. It is true this old man is dried up, like one in the desert, yet still he lives to drink his chai and beat boys with his camel stick. But no longer does he hold the head of the camel when it is in line for racing. Breath of Dog is doing this now. He is the son of Old Goat's cousin and he is a bad man. It is because of him Yasub is dead now.

Old Goat curses me. "Ah, Allah! Why are you punishing me with this lazy boy? I am wanting chai before saying my prayers, and now there is not time enough. Say your prayers quickly now, and then go to boil water so it is hot when I finish mine."

I turn in the direction of Mecca and kneel with my forehead touching the ground. But instead of saying my prayers, I look up between my hands to the tall tower of Abudai. It is a building that stands bigger than all others in the city, and my mama said to me that every morning, when the sun rises, before she is starting work for a rich sheikh in Abudai, she also would look toward this tower. She said it would help her to know that I would also be looking—that even though we couldn't see each other, we would never be far apart as long as we could both see this same thing.

But this morning its dark shape is like a shadow because I feel so much sadness. I am sad that I am not waking in my home in Bangladesh with my babu and mama, just like in my dreams. I am here, still, in this hot desert land where the sand is grey and drifting with the wind.

I am not wanting the tears to come, for never am I crying. Not since Babu told me to be like a man and never cry. And I do not. Not even when Babu is dying or when Mama is leaving me with the *dalals*, the slave traders, who brought me to this camp to live. I do not cry when Old Goat is screeching or when Breath of Dog is beating me. Not even when I fall from the camel and lose the tooths in my head. Never am I crying. It is just these foolish dreams that make me remember a time before I came here. Before I became a camel rider.

As I rise, I quickly touch my cheeks. My face grows hot, for it is as I feared. There is wetness.

"Always crying for his mama in the darkness." Old Goat puts his face close to mine. "He is too much like one *bint*." He spits, and slaps my face. The blow is stinging to my cheeks.

Suddenly the redness of anger is upon me.

I leap at Old Goat and bite his arm. As he squeals like a goat with its throat being slit, I hear the early morning call to prayer.

CHAPTER THREE ADAM
DAWN IN ABUDAI, DAY ONE

Even in my dreams I hear the wailing call to pre-dawn prayers from all the nearby mosques and then the beep-beeping of my alarm clock. Then I realize I'm not dreaming anymore. I'm awake. When I open my eyes, I see that it's 4:30 in the morning. I press the button on the alarm to stop it beeping and wish there was a button I could press to stop all the *Allah Akbar*-ing. That's one thing I will be pleased about, with going back to Australia. I won't have to listen to "God is Great" being blasted from every mosque five times a day.

It does finally stop, and all I can hear is the hum of the air conditioner as it kicks in to keep the house at the constant, freezing temperature that my mum insists on. Sometimes it's so cold inside and so hot outside that the windows stream with condensation, just like it's raining. Of course, it's not. It only rains a couple of times a year in the city. It's great when it does, because it's usually a big storm and the water is all over the road. Me and my mates get on our bikes and ride through it and make the biggest waves. The best storms, though, are in the mountains in the summertime. There was a picture in the paper of water taller than me coming down a *wadi*, which is a dried-up creek bed. I wish I'd been there with my surfboard. It would have been awesome.

But there's not likely to be any rain today. Grey light comes through the arched window of my huge bedroom. When we first came to live here, we couldn't believe the size of the houses and the rooms, but the Arabs like to build massive houses out of all this poured concrete. The walls are really thick to keep the heat out and the cool of the air-conditioning in. And you need the space because you have to spend a lot of time inside. As usual, my room's a mess, but I don't care. Chandra will clean it up.

That thought gets me moving. Chandra will be up soon, and I want to make the most of today. I need to be gone before she realizes I'm awake. Not that it's a big deal, really, because no matter what my mum thinks, I do what I like when there's only

Chandra here. But Chandra cries if I don't do what she tells me. She thinks Mum will tell her off. Really it would be me Mum'd get stuck into; still, it's easier just to go. That way Chandra's too scared to tell Mum what I've done, and I won't have to see Chandra cry.

I hear Tara thumping her tail, and I feel her long, cold, black nose on my face. Tara's my dog, and she sleeps in my room. She's just the right height to be able to give me a lick without having to jump up onto the bed. If I wasn't properly awake before, I am now.

"Hey, girl," I say, as I sit upright. "We're going surfing."

I pull on an old T-shirt and my favorite shorts— the pair my mum hates because she says they drag around my bum and dag around my knees. She says I look like I've grown up in a gutter or something, instead of having all the privileges other boys my age would give their right arm for, et cetera, et cetera, et cetera.

I've heard it so many times before. "You're too spoilt," she says. Blah, blah, blah. That's when I turn right off. All I want to do is surf and hang out with my mates. Nearly everyone in our group came here at about the same time when their dads, like mine, got a job with the new airline. We all come from different places—Australia, England, Canada, Kenya,

Belgium, Spain and New Zealand, too. When we were young we used to call ourselves the Compound Kids. Now we just call ourselves the Sea Ks, which sort of still stands for Compound Kids, but also means Sea Kings. That's what we are.

My mum reckons it's been good for my development to go to an International School with lots of kids from other countries. But when I ask why I can't stay here, she says I'll end up an expat for the rest of my days if I don't know where my real home is. But this *is* home. And Nigel and Jean-Marie and Bud and Nelson and Jose and Jason are my mates.

I don't even mind that it's so hot here. And it *is* hot. Hotter than Hell. I'm not supposed to swear. But how can "Hell" be a proper swearword when it's supposed to be a place? And seriously, even Hell couldn't be as hot as it is here in summer.

It's late August now. But it's been hot since May and it won't cool down until October. Most people hate the summer in Abudai because it's over 40°C every day and it never gets cool outside. You have to live in air-conditioning all the time. And I don't even need to be told to cover myself with sunscreen. You can get burned really quickly.

I smear the sticky cream all over my face and arms and legs and then put another thick blob on my nose to make sure. I cram the bottle into my back pocket and grab my favorite cap. Mum's always worrying I'll end up with heatstroke riding my bike to the beach and back. The sun does beat down a bit, but as long as we get back before about midday it's not too bad.

Apart from the sunburn, I like the summer because it means we get extra long holidays. If I was allowed to stay here, I would still have three weeks of holidays left and then I'd be going into my first year at Abudai Secondary College. That's where all my mates are going. I've tried to tell Mum and Dad that going back to Australia isn't fair. I'll have to do half a year more at school than anyone else because school here started in September last year and finished in June this year. Back in Australia they'll only be halfway through the year. And I won't know anybody. And I'll miss Tara. It's not fair! I want to stay here.

"Come on, girl," I call softly to Tara, but she just flicks one ear.

"We're going surfing," I say again. That usually gets her excited, but she still doesn't move. In the grey light, I can see her outline. Some people say she's a funny-looking dog, but I think she's beautiful. I have to admit she doesn't look like any other dog I know, but that's because she's a "bitsa"—with bitsa this and bitsa that in her. She's got tall, skinny legs like a desert dog, a long pointy nose like a wolfhound, and a black coat like a Labrador. And she's got the biggest ears. They look like radars. It wouldn't surprise me if she could pick up messages from airplanes flying overhead with those ears. And she's definitely one smart dog. She knows exactly what's going on, all the time.

With her ears up and angled out she looks just like these dog mummies we saw in a museum in Egypt when Mum and Dad and Sarah and I went over there for a holiday. They say the ancient Egyptians used to love their dogs so much that when a dog died, everyone shaved off their eyebrows. How cool is that?

Sarah bought a little statue of one of those dogs while we were there because she said it looked just like Tara. It does, too, and Sarah took it back to boarding school with her. She said it meant she could have Tara looking after her there.

Tara is good at guarding. She sits by the gate and watches everyone like that's her job. I reckon Tara's great-great-great-hundreds-of-great-grandfather would've sat outside some pharaoh's temple and kept tomb robbers away.

"What can you hear, girl?" I ask. Tara suddenly rushes to the door barking like there's something out there she wants to chase.

"Tara!" I yell over her barking, to try and shut her up. I don't need her to wake Chandra up. Or half the compound, either.

Then there's a noise so loud it drowns out my yell. It even drowns out Tara's barking.

It's like thunder. But I know it can't be thunder. There might be storms in the mountains at this time of year, but not here on the coast. Not here.

Then, out of nowhere, comes a whining roar. It's like a swarm of giant, angry mosquitoes.

I know that sound. I was born at a military air base. My dad was a pilot in the air force before we came over here. I recognize that crackling noise.

Military planes, igniting their afterburners.

Waves of them begin to scream overhead. Must be only about thirty meters above the ground by the noise they're making and the shuddering I can feel. My ears are ringing. I can see Tara opening her mouth, but I can't hear her barking any more. I know she is, though. She's not scared of anything: not fire-crackers or thunder. She just wants to protect our family.

I can't work out what's going on. Why would planes like these be coming over so low at this time of the morning? I figure it must be some sort of military exercise so I run out onto the balcony, which faces the outside of the compound. I want a good view of this show!

They're coming from the direction of the coast and they're flying very low—not much higher than our rooftop as they swoop away.

I recognize the shape of them. Phantoms! But nobody has Phantoms nowadays. They're really old technology. Nobody except the Sultan of Mafi, who's in charge of a small country to the south of here. But what are they doing having a military exercise in Abudai?

Then, from the direction of the desert, I see a scramble of Abudai Tomcats. Wow!

The Phantoms head straight for the Centra Tower, the tallest building in Abudai. They look as if they're going to hit about the tenth floor, but they pull up and go over it. And then it's like bits start falling off the wings. Long, black, egg-shaped bits.

I know what they are, but I can't believe what's happening.

The top of the Centra explodes. The noise is huge. In movies things like this happen in slow motion. But all I can see is stuff flying upwards and out, like it's being thrown up by some gigantic hand.

It happens quickly. Too quickly.

Holy Hell! They're dropping bombs.

CHAPTER FOUR WALID
DAWN IN THE DESERT, DAY ONE

"*Halas!* Finish!" A voice is bawling louder than a bull camel. It is Breath of Dog at the doorway of the hut where he and Old Goat sleep.

I have not taken water for him to wash before prayers. For this he will be angry—and for waking him with so much noise. I can see the darkness in his eyes as he wraps his *doti* around him, the cloth tight around his bulging belly. He strides towards us.

Now, I am thinking, is a good time to run fast away, for with this call to prayer Old Goat and Breath of Dog must stop all things, even beatings, to be saying prayers.

I dodge under the arm of Old Goat, jump over the

heads of Badir and Mustapha who are crying. Like babies, they are always frightened.

"What is this loud disturbance?" yells Breath of Dog.

"It is being Walid's fault."

As I run from the yard, I hear Badir and Mustapha squealing like rats. I want to spit on them! I hate them! Breath of Dog favors them because they are small and light and the camel does not feel their weight upon its back, which is why, in the races, they come in front of me. Always they are mocking me, calling out, "Camel Shanks, Camel Shanks, always in the last ranks."

I know my legs are long and skinny and, in truthfulness, looking like those of a camel. But I do not know why, because even when I am so hungry, I do not eat all my daily roti and rice. Yet still I am growing.

I do not want to grow and become too heavy on the back of a camel, for then it will never win any race. And I must win. Even just one big race, for then I will earn many dirhams, much money. Then my mama and I can go back to Bangladesh.

If Babu were alive, we would be there still. After he got the sickness in his chest and died, Mama paid all our rupees to the *dalals* for buying passports so we could come to this country. They told my mama that if I am a good little boy, smart little boy, then I will learn reading and writing and very soon, I would become rich like a sheikh. I was very proud when I heard this. I promised Mama that I would be the best camel rider in the world.

"Always Walid!" I hear Breath of Dog snort. "For sure, I will give you one hell of a beating after the praying. Too much! You will be crying for your mama."

"I am never crying!" I yell. When the flames of anger leap in my chest, then no tears can come. "You will never catch me for I am running fast away."

"Ha!" roars Breath of Dog. "The police will catch you and they will give you one hell of a thrashing and put you in prison."

"And Allah will cast your soul into the pits of Hell to burn forever for not saying your prayers," screams Old Goat.

"I am not scared of police or Hell or anything," I yell, but it is not the truth. Sometimes, at night, before I am sleeping, I am being very frightened of the punishment of Allah for not always saying prayers and for being bad like Old Goat is always saying.

"Before you run fast away, see to the camels," shouts Breath of Dog.

The camels! I cannot run away, for then who would care for the camels? Especially Shirin, with her eyes that have the softness of ripened dates. Gentle Shirin, whose name means "sweet." Who would help her when she is ready to calve? Very soon, she will need me to carry soft hay for her to lie on when she brings this new calf into the world. As I think of Shirin, the redness of my anger soaks away, like the water in the sands.

I will untie the hobbles on Shirin so she can move

more easily, so she can find the sweetest grasses further away. Breath of Dog will be angry. He never unties the hobbles, for he says the camels will roam too far. But already he is angry, and I will get a beating so it is no matter. I know Shirin will return when I call her.

Every morning, the camels greet me with eagerness to be freed from the pen where they are kept at night, but as I pull back the gate of woven palm fronds they are looking in the other direction, towards the desert.

"My beauties! My pets! My gentlenesses! My joys!" I call. Shirin, who is the most special to me, turns her long neck and snickers, but there is a fearfulness in the sound. I run to her.

"What is wrong?" I ask, as I reach up and scratch the bumpy knob on her forehead. "Is this calf making a pain in your belly? A small walk and sweet grasses will help." I rub her stomach. So big now is the calf inside her that her skin is stretched too tightly. She moans softly as I kneel down to unbind her feet, but the knots are tight. Finally, I release her.

"Ah, there. Thank Allah!"

As I say this, there is suddenly a noise of tremendous greatness. The air shudders. Above my head, too many airplanes come flying. So close. My ears hurt with the crackling roar. They fly towards Abudai like giant bats.

All the camels are startled, but they are hobbled so cannot move far. All except Shirin. She kicks up her feet and runs away over the dunes.

"Shirin! *La!* No!" I yell, and run after her. She is too heavy and there are many holes in the ground—she will trip and break her leg.

"Allah, have mercy!" I hear Old Goat behind me. From the direction of Abudai I hear a rumbling, and the earth beneath my feet shakes. At the same moment, I see Shirin lurch forwards.

"Allah! *La!*"

Then, as Shirin crashes down, I hear a sound like the snapping of a branch that has been dried by many summers in the burning sun. Her fearful screaming is like a knife wound in my heart.

"This is war!" I hear Breath of Dog yell. And when I turn away from the sight of Shirin lying with the white bone sticking out from her leg, I see, in the distance, the top of the tall tower of Abudai explode.

CHAPTER FIVE ADAM
JUST AFTER DAWN IN ABUDAI, DAY ONE

"What's happening?" That's our standard Sea K greeting, but everyone in the compound is yelling it now.

I can hear them as I run down the stairs and push open the big sliding glass doors in our sitting room, the ones that lead straight into the communal garden. There are about fifty people out there already. Most of them are still in their dressing gowns.

Somebody's got to know what's going on. But I look around and listen to what they're saying, and nobody seems to know what's happening at all.

"It's the Iraqis," I hear Mr. Walker, from two doors down, saying.

Dumbo. Iraqis don't have Phantoms.

"It must just be an exercise," says Mr. Lemere, Jean-Marie's dad.

Yeah, right. Some exercise, when they blow the top off the Centra Tower.

"I knew it would happen one day."

"Is it an invasion?"

"We'll have to get out of here before they round us up."

Mr. Bigg, Nigel's dad, is trying to organize everybody to head off through the mountains to Suman.

For some dumb reason I think about Sarah. She'll go green when she hears about this. She's obsessed with being a journalist. Not long after we arrived, the first summer when it was a bit boring here, Mum suggested she start up a newspaper in the compound. Sarah got right into it. She called it the Compound Network News—CNN. She used to go around and try to dig up interesting information and she'd interview people and stuff. Dad even made her a special press badge with a string and everything. She thought it was pretty cool and wore it around her neck just like the reporters on TV. This'd make the CNN headlines for sure. Hell, it's even going to make the real CNN news. "Centra Tower Bombed!" is a bit more interesting than "Missing Cat!" or "Hot Water Tank Bursts in Number 3!"

Then I see my friend, Jason, who lives three doors down. He's in his jocks and a singlet and he's shaking, although it's not cold. Jason's a Kiwi. He and I are the only Sea Ks here right now. His mum doesn't like to go home at this time of year because she says New Zealand's too cold. But my other friends—Nigel, Jean-Marie, Bud, Jose, and Nelson—are all away for the summer.

Jason's not, like, my best friend or anything. He's a bit too much of a show-off sometimes, but he's okay. I go over to talk to him, hoping I don't look as white as he does.

"Hey!" I say. Then, at the same time, we both say, "What's happening, man?"

There might only be the two of us, but we're still Sea Ks; we're still cool. Jason grins, but his eyes look frightened. Then, I can't help it, I start to giggle.

"What's so funny?" he asks. I can't reply because I don't really know. It's nothing and everything. Crazy things. I point to Mr. Bigg who's bossing everyone around. He's just wearing his boxer shorts with little devils on them and his stomach is hanging in rolls over the waistband. Jason starts to giggle, too.

"And look at old Mrs. Vane," he splutters. "You can see her black lacy nightie underneath that leopard-print thing she's got wrapped around her."

Then, in the distance, there's a rumbling noise.

"That's tanks," Jason says, sounding half-scared and half-excited and all know-it-all. Like he's the only one who can tell what the noise is.

"Yeah, I know . . ." I begin to say, but there's a volley of shots that sound really close. We can hear men shouting in Arabic. Mrs. Vane screams and starts to cry loudly, and that sets some of the little kids off. Somebody else swears and says we're all going to die. Then everybody starts either yelling orders or asking questions.

"We're not staying around here."

"We'll travel in convoy."

"Can I take my hamster?"

"Just hurry!"

"Will we be able to get petrol when we get over the border?"

"We'll need water."

"Can we still get money out of the cash machines?"

"I don't know! I don't know!"

"Stop crying! Don't panic!"

"I want to go home!"

It's weird seeing everyone looking so scared, especially when they're only wearing their dressing gowns and pajamas. I'm glad I'm dressed. I still want to laugh, which is freaky because I don't really think anything is funny at all.

"This is no joking matter, Adam." I'm almost stunned by a whack around the ears. It's Mr. Hartliss. His wife, Margot, is Mum's best friend in the compound, but I don't like them much. They know my mum flew out last night and that my dad won't be back until tonight.

"You'd better come with us." Mr. Hartliss frowns at me. "I don't know how we're going to get you over the border without a passport, but I guess with what's going on here that shouldn't be a major problem. Now, quickly go and grab some clothes, and some food and drink, and put everything in a bag. Make sure you bring plenty of water. Be back down outside as quickly as you can."

I run into the house and call out for Chandra. But there's no answer. I swear. Loudly. She's either taken off to her friend's place or she's hiding and is too scared to come out. Pathetic!

I hear Tara scratching at my bedroom door. I must have accidentally shut her in when I raced downstairs. I go up and let her out. She whimpers and cringes like it's all her fault.

"It's okay. It's okay," I say to her. But it's not okay and she knows it. I pat her and gently pull her warm ears, which are silky and smooth.

But I can't spend all day patting Tara. I've got to get some stuff. Tara watches me as I upend my clothes drawers: T-shirts, shorts, jocks, and socks spill out onto the floor. I dump all the books out of my school backpack. I'm definitely not taking them with me. With any luck they'll get blown up.

Before I lose it totally, I stuff my clothes into the bag, and I remember Mr. Hartliss said I had to get some food and drink. I race back down to the kitchen. I grab three tins of dog food for Tara, then I go to the fridge. The first thing I see is the box of After-Dinner Mints that Mum keeps for when she has people over for dinner. Chocolate's food. I grab the box and a big bottle of Coke, plus a wad of cheese slices. I give Tara one. She loves cheese. I rummage around, but there's nothing else, only lettuce, some carrots, tomatoes, a couple of avocados, heaps of half-empty bottles of jam and chutney, half a container of milk and a plate of leftovers. Our fridge is always boring.

Mr. Hartliss said to get lots of water so I grab the last three bottles of mineral water from the box under the stairs and stuff them in my bag as well. Then I remember Dad's thermos water bottle he carries with him when he goes walking. Because the water will stay cold, I fill up the bottle with icy water from the drink fountain. And it's got a strap, so I sling it around my neck and under my arm. I feel like I'm going exploring.

As I grab the house keys out of the drawer, I see an envelope with the two hundred dirhams that my mum leaves for Chandra in case of emergencies. Nobody can say this isn't an emergency.

I take the bundle, which is in a great wad of five and ten dirham notes and cram it into my pocket alongside my Swiss Army knife and my mobile.

I guess it's kinda dumb to take the mobile because it's only one of those "pay as you go" sorts. Mum wouldn't trust me with it otherwise. It's probably only got about ten or twenty dirhams left on it so it won't get me far, and the battery's low as well. I always forget to charge it. Maybe I'll call Jason from the Hartlisses' four-wheel drive. That'd be cool. I grab Dad's special charger, which you can use in the lighter of a car. Maybe Mr. Hartliss will let me charge up my phone while we're traveling.

"Come on, girl," I say to Tara as I pull the heavy, wooden door closed and lock it. Tara is starting to get excited now. She loves going out in the car. "We're going on an adventure."

I see the Hartlisses' white Range Rover and we run toward it. The three Hartliss girls, who are much younger than me, are sitting in the backseat with their seat belts on. They've all got blond hair and I can barely tell them apart. They're in their nighties.

Briefly, I hope I don't have to squeeze up with them. Any girl is bad enough, but these girls are the worst. They're just so . . . so girly. I'd prefer to sit behind the backseat with Tara.

Mr. and Mrs. Hartliss come out lugging a wooden chest between them. It's huge.

"That cost over five thousand dirhams. I'm not leaving it behind. I've put our clothes in it," Mrs. Hartliss tells me, even though I don't care. Then I realize I'm expected to squash up next to it and I do care. Tara and I won't be able to move.

"But you can't take the dog," Mrs. Hartliss says. "Shelly's allergic to animal dander. Remember? We had to give away our cat. Besides, there's no room for an animal."

"We are not taking a dog over the border anyway," Mr. Hartliss adds.

"But you've got to take her," I say desperately. "I can't leave her behind. She hasn't even had breakfast."

"Sorry, Adam," says Mr. Hartliss not sounding sorry at all. "It's just not possible."

"Then I'm not going either," I say.

"I've had enough of this nonsense." Mr. Hartliss sounds angry. "Get in the car now!"

"But I can't leave Tara. She'll be killed," I scream at him. I'm angry now, and I've got a fierce temper. My mum says it comes with the red hair and Irish ancestors.

"We haven't got time to argue." Mr. Hartliss sounds really mad at me now.

I can see the convoy's already started. Tara, with her tail and ears down, takes off like she always does when people start arguing. She goes and crawls under a bush and lies with her nose between her paws.

She'll stay there until somebody tells her it's alright.

I bolt after her, but Mr. Hartliss is fast. He grabs my arm and drags me back, then pushes me into the back of the truck. He slams the door and locks it so I can't jump out.

I see Jason trying to grin at me from the front seat of his family's Nissan Patrol, which is right behind us, but it's all a blur because of the hot, fat tears sliding out of my eyes. I don't even care that everyone can see me crying.

CHAPTER SIX WALID
AFTER DAWN IN THE DESERT, DAY ONE

"To Hell you are going!" Breath of Dog is tying my hands and my feet with Shirin's hobbles. He ties them tight and then picks up his gun.

With his gun he has made Shirin dead. Her leg was broken and she could never again be running in races. Then he slit her belly to get the calf, but that, too, was dead.

"*Ana as if. Ana as if.* I am sorry," I whisper over and over, after the last shudders of Shirin, and after her spilled blood has soaked into the sand. I cannot stop shaking. In my belly there is a hardness like one dried-up, knotted coconut rope.

"It is too late for sorriness now," says Old Goat, pinching my arm hard. "For this deed you will pay."

"Say your prayers," yells Breath of Dog, lifting his gun. "Because to Hell I am sending you."

Many times before, Old Goat has said that when I die I will go straight to Hell for all my badness. Is it my badness that has made all this happen? Instead of looking at the tall tower and thinking of Mama, I should have been saying my prayers. Now Allah has taken away my Shirin, and the Abudai tower. Truly this is punishment enough, but Breath of Dog is too angry. Is it the will of Allah that I should die also? I lean my head on the body of Shirin. I cannot be running fast away from this punishment.

"No shooting," says Old Goat. "For with the shooting the police will come."

"But he untied the hobbles of this camel. A good racing camel! She was worth many dirhams." Breath of Dog is yelling so much I see the gold tooth in his head glinting, and in his eyes is the fury of blood.

"Yes, yes," Old Goat is saying. "It is true that this boy needs punishing and this we will give him. But not by killing him, for we can sell him and make some money."

"Pshaw!" hisses Breath of Dog. "Who would want this useless camel *walid?*"

"We can sell him back to the *dalals* who will send him to make carpets in the factories," says Old Goat. "We can get maybe five hundred dirhams for him."

There is the light of greed in Breath of Dog's eyes and then it dies.

"But with this war starting, how can we find the dalals?"

"Ah, true," says Old Goat. "Maybe we should just dump him in the mountains. He has proved to be a bad investment after all."

"It would be easier to shoot him," says Breath of Dog.

"Yes, yes," says Old Goat. "But there is a risk. We want no problem with the police. No, it is better to take him to that Hell on Earth and leave him there."

As Breath of Dog grunts and nods, I see that it is not Allah's will that I die today. Now, suddenly, I am so relieved. I do not want to die. Then, Breath of Dog picks me up and throws me into the back of the Toyota truck.

"To Hell you are going."

This Hell on Earth is far away and along a jolting road, and all the time I am thinking. Babu told me that always we must submit our will to Allah, but I remember how angry he was in his sickness and how, sometimes, he cursed even the will of Allah when he fought to have breath in his body. He told me that to feel anger is better than to let fear into the heart.

I curse also.

"This one likes fighting too much," says Old Goat, turning and prodding me with his camel stick. "Maybe we can sell him to be a soldier, now there is this war in Abudai."

Breath of Dog spits out the window and then turns and slaps my head. He hits me so hard my nose bleeds, and I cannot yell and breathe at the same time.

Breath of Dog spits again. "I am thinking this war will

be over quickly," he says. "For all the sheikhs in this country are too soft. They will be running fast away and never fighting."

"But it is not the sheikhs who will be fighting," says Old Goat. "For they will be quickly calling their American friends who will come with their big warplanes." He makes a clicking sound with his fingers. "The war will then be finished. *Halas!*"

Breath of Dog, finally, stops the truck. "Ah," he says. "This will do."

I feel the shaking inside my stomach. I do not want to be in this Hell on Earth. I try to curse, but my mouth is dry. Breath of Dog opens the truck door, picks me up and throws me over his shoulder.

I know straight away that this is one bad place. It is hotter even than the desert, and there is no wind. But I do not see black devils or leaping flames devouring the souls of all the wicked people, as in the stories Old Goat is always telling me. There is only quietness in this Hell. And mountainous grey rocks.

As Breath of Dog climbs the steep slope, small stones roll away down the hill. If only I had a sharp rock, I could cut these ropes that bind me.

"*Bas!* The end!" Breath of Dog suddenly flings me into a shadowy cave in the side of the mountain. This Hell on Earth is hard, for when my head hits the ground there is only blackness.

CHAPTER SEVEN ADAM
EARLY MORNING IN THE MOUNTAINS, DAY ONE

We made it over the border. Even me, with no pass-port. There was a bit of a hassle, of course, but every-one was nervous. I guess the customs people didn't want to be stuck with a nearly-thirteen-year-old boy with no passport, so in the end they just waved us through. They had other things to worry about.

I wish they had stopped me. I want to get back to Abudai to rescue Tara. She'll die without anybody to feed her. Plus the Arabs hate dogs. I try not to think about the fact that the compound might get bombed.

I spent the hour it took driving to the border cry-ing and kicking the door of the car. Mr. Hartliss was mad as hell, but I didn't care. He kept threatening to put me out, but I knew he wouldn't because at last we found out what's going on; there have been announcements on the radio.

Most of what they said was in Arabic, but every now and then they'd make an announcement in English. I'd figured most of it out already. Like, I already knew it had to be the SOM (Sultanate of Mafi) forces. They say they've taken over Abudai at the request of their Arab brothers who believe that the city has become too open to corrupt western influences.

Now our little convoy of corrupt forces has stopped at a petrol station just over the border. Apart from the fact that everyone's really nervy and wants to get going as quickly as possible, it's weird how normal everything still is.

I hop out of the car and can feel how hot it is already as I look around at the steep, bare, rocky slopes of the Fahaj Mountains. My dad says they look like a moonscape. Usually when we come for a drive to the mountains, I like watching the peaks appear over the horizon. Their jagged shapes rise up at the edge of the orange desert. They look like the Mountains of Doom from this video game I have. They're like the Mountains of Doom, too, because nothing much grows on them except small thorny bushes, which only goats and camels can eat.

And they suit my mood now, because I feel as if I am doomed. How can everything have gone so wrong, so quickly?

"Why's he crying all the time?" I hear one of the girls ask her mother.

"Cos he had to leave his dog at home," says the eldest super-pain-in-the-neck one.

"I hope you're going to act your age now, Adam," says Mrs. Hartliss. "We're all a little scared, you know. And it doesn't help you throwing a tantrum because you can't have what you want. Look at my girls. They're being brave."

"Yeah," I mutter, thinking that I want to kill them all and save the SOM troops the trouble.

"Maybe you'd like to travel the rest of the way to Suman with one of your other friends," Mrs. Hartliss suggests.

Yeah, I know they just want to get rid of me. Well, I don't want to spend another four or five hours with them, either. Then it suddenly hits me. Another brilliant plan.

"Can I go in my friend Jason's car from here?" I ask Mr. Hartliss, who's just finished checking the tires and oil and stuff.

"Good idea," he says, sounding relieved as he follows Mrs. Hartliss into the shop to buy some more water.

It's too easy, I think, as I grab my bag by the

shoulder strap and head towards the toilets around the side of the shop. Hopefully no one will notice I'm not in any of the cars.

The whole service station is built to look like a fake mountain fortress and the toilets are small round forts. They look just like the sandcastle towers kids make on the beach. Although it's only about 6:30 a.m., it's already hot and I'm pleased to reach the shade of these fake forts, although I'm not thrilled with the pong.

I go into a cubicle and wade through the puddle on the floor. There's no real toilet—just a hole in the tiled floor. That's how they do it here—squatting.

I hear the cars starting up. The sound is loud, even here in the toilets. I get this sick feeling in my stomach. Like maybe this isn't such a brilliant plan. My heart starts to beat more quickly and I feel sweat dribbling down under my armpits. I want to rush out and tell them to wait for me, but I stop myself.

I have to go back and rescue Tara. I can't just leave her there.

She'll die.

I hear the cars rumble away.

Then there's silence.

I wait for a bit. They didn't really leave without me. They wouldn't. Somebody will come in and drag me out in a minute and blast me.

It gets hotter. All I can hear is the wind whistling

as it blows through the small arched windows near the ceiling.

Maybe they're waiting for me to come out. Then they'll give me a good telling off. I unlock the door and peer around. They've gone. It's like the cars and everyone in them have vanished in the swirl of dust I can see rising between the petrol pumps. There's only a stain spreading on the asphalt where the air conditioner of someone's car has leaked to show the convoy was here at all. They've really gone.

Holy Hell! They've gone and left me behind.

For a minute I feel like crying, I'm so scared. As I step back into the toilet and lock the door again, I can feel myself shaking and I begin to get mad.

The bastards! The bloody bastards! I'm so angry at Mr. Hartliss for being horrible and bossy and making me leave Tara behind. I had no choice except to run away. And while I'm at it, I'm mad at Mrs. Hartliss for only caring about those three idiot girls of hers and that stupid wooden chest, and at Jason and Mrs. Vane and everybody else for not noticing I wasn't in any of the cars. How could they just leave me here? Why didn't they do a head count? I was only in the toilet. They should have guessed I might try something. They know I got myself left behind last night. And what if I hadn't planned it? I could have just had a stomachache. They didn't even notice someone was missing. Shows how much they care. I can feel the tears sliding down my cheeks again and I can taste the saltiness in my mouth. They can all go and get . . . get . . . stuffed.

Tara's the only one who cares about me and I'm going to go back and rescue her.

In the silence I hear the squeak of sneakers on concrete. The door handle rattles. Suddenly, I feel really scared. Who is it? What do they want? I try to tell my brain it's just one of the attendants wanting to go to the toilet. I stay as quiet as I can, but I'm starting to panic. Why the hell did I get myself into this? I don't even breathe.

The handle rattles again and I hear a soft muttering, but I can't tell if it's Arabic or Urdu—the language the Pakistanis speak here. Then I hear cars pull up, honking their horns. I hear the feet move away and I breathe out. I almost shout out loud I'm so pleased. It must be the Hartlisses or somebody, coming back to pick me up. Quickly I unlock the door and step out.

But I don't recognize any of the cars in this convoy, and they've nearly all got tinted windows. Men in traditional clothing—*dishdash*—get out of the cars and talk to each other. Locals. I step back into the toilet and lock the door again. What am I going to do? I try to think. Do I go out and ask for their help? What if they don't speak English? And would they care anyway?

Luckily no one in this convoy seems to need to use the toilet, but I know I can't keep myself locked up here forever. And I can't just appear out of nowhere, either. The service station attendants will see me and want to know what's going on. I mean, I'm a westerner and over here that means you're somebody.

But what am I going to do? Wait for the next group of westerners to come along? When I catch up with the Hartlisses, I'll get a super blasting for getting myself left behind again. And what about Tara? I still have to save her. But I can't just march back down the road. I'll never get over the border again without a passport. The soldiers have got guns. This time they'll probably just shoot me so they don't have to bother about me. I think they're pretty ruthless out here.

My mind is racing with thoughts, each getting more dramatic than the one before. Of course, I don't really believe they'll kill me, but you never know.

It's getting hotter by the minute. I glance at my watch and I'm surprised. It's only just after 7:00 a.m. But it feels much later.

I finally realize there's only one thing to do. I'll have to head off into the mountains and work out the way back to Abudai from there, because I have to go back and rescue Tara now, no matter what. Whichever way I look at it, I'm in big trouble, so I may as well make it worthwhile.

I wait until the cars have left and there's silence again. The attendants have all disappeared back into the air-conditioned shop. I don't blame them for that.

As I step out with my water bottle under my arm and backpack slung over my back, I pull my cap down so the peak covers my face. I keep close to the wall. The heat from the ground reflects up at me. The sun is well above the surrounding peaks and it's already white hot. I quickly look around to work out which way to go.

A high concrete wall runs around three sides of the service station. Once I can get down behind that, I'll be safe from being seen. Then it's not far to a goat track I can see that winds up between the mountains. It's sort of going at right angles to the road, but that's okay. When I get far enough in, I'll turn toward Abudai again.

There are dried-up *wadis* winding through the mountains; the Bedu drive along them and use them as roads. I can follow one of them. Hey! That's it! There'll be Bedu out there I can hitch a ride with. They might not want to drive into Abudai with the invasion on, but for two hundred dirhams they'll get me to the camel camps near the outskirts of the town at least.

Of course, my Arabic is not too good. We had to

learn it for a year at school so I know greetings and numbers and a few words, but it was never my favorite class. The thing is, you don't have to speak the language to live here because everyone seems to speak English. And anyway, money talks. I'm pleased I was smart enough to put that emergency money in my pocket now. This could be a real adventure.

Now I've got a plan, I feel great again. And besides, if it all gets too much or I can't hitch a ride, I'll just come back here and ask the attendants for help. They'll look after me until somebody in the convoy figures out I've been left behind.

But I've got to give this plan a go. For Tara's sake.

Just as I prepare to rush across the few meters of open space between the toilet and the wall, a man in the red uniform of the service station walks around the corner of the shop. He's carrying a bucket of dirty water. He stops.

For what seems like forever, we just stare at each other. Then the man grunts as he turns and throws the water away. It's like I'm not even there. I watch him as he walks back around the corner. Westerner or not—he doesn't want to know. I'm on my own.

Still in shock, I sprint towards the wall and clamber over it. It's about a two-meter drop down the other side and I skin my knee as I jump to the ground.

The scrape stings like crazy, but there's not much

blood. I half-wish I'd hurt myself a bit more so I'd have a good excuse not to keep going; when I look up at the bare, rocky peaks of the mountains, I feel a cold shiver run through me, despite the heat from the sun hammering down on the baked, hard land.

PART TWO
DESERT

CHAPTER EIGHT
EARLY AFTERNOON, DAY ONE

I'm dripping. I drag my eyelids up like I'm lifting a heavy weight, but the glare of the sun is like a laser beam drilling holes in my head. It makes me blink and close my eyes again straight away. Suddenly the ground is rising up to hit me.

It hits me hard enough to wake me. But I don't wake up.

That must mean I am asleep and this is a dream. Soon Mum will call me to get up and then Tara will put her cold, wet nose in my face. I can hear the thumping of her tail. No. The thumping is in my head. This isn't a dream, is it?

No. It's a nightmare. It must be, because otherwise

I'm lost in the middle of a baked world of bare, rocky peaks with the white hot sun crawling like a glowing snail across a sky that looks like it's made of tin.

But all those awful things couldn't really have happened. There can't have been an invasion with bombings and soldiers shooting. And I wouldn't have been so stupid that I deliberately got myself left behind at a service station in the middle of nowhere. That service station's just vanished now. Like it was only a mirage.

I've walked back for kilometers, but it's not there anymore. I guess it's because I'm so confused with all these valleys and dried-up *wadis* going in all directions.

I have to drag myself up and try to pull myself together or I'll never get out of here. I look at my watch. It's after midday. I've been walking for hours. If only I could find my way back to that service station. Or if only somebody would come along and rescue me. But there's nobody here. It's silent. And hot. Too hot even for the birds.

I need to talk to somebody. Anybody. I've tried every number I've got punched into my mobile, but all I'm getting is either "the mobile phone you are calling is switched off or out of range" or a message telling me to leave a message. I do. I've even tried to ring Mum, but she'll still be in the air somewhere.

It's the only time she has it switched off. Not like my dad. He never turns his on.

I know I'm running out of credit and the battery indicator on my mobile is getting lower. I have to switch it off before it dies. I feel like parts of me are switching off, too. My legs aren't moving too well anymore, and my head feels as if it's become swollen and too heavy for my body to carry.

I take my hat off to fan myself. The hat's stiff with sweat and sunscreen; it's probably kept most of the sun off my face. And it was lucky I put in the tube of sunscreen. It's all gone now, though. I keep sweating it off.

I need another drink. But I've drunk the three bottles of water and I've finished off the Coke, which was horrible because it was sticky and warm. I know I should have been more careful with the water, but I had to drink it—otherwise I'm sure I'd be dead by now. I even tipped the last of the cold water over my head when it felt like it was going to split if I didn't wet it.

I really need a drink. But the weird part is, I feel like I'm looking at the world through water. Everything's moving, swaying like the weeds in our fish tank. Am I in a fish tank?

No, I can't be, because then I would be cool and wet. I know! The world is in the fish tank and I'm the only thing outside it. Looking in. I'm the only living being in this hot, waterless world. Outside everything. Really on my own. Forever.

Thinking makes me feel dizzy. I sit down before I fall again, and I lean back against the steep slope of a ridge. In a few hours, the sun will be behind it and at least there'll be some shade here. I just can't move anymore. I close my eyes, listening to the silence. Then I hear the sound of small stones rolling down the side of the slope.

There must be an animal up there. I'm not on my own after all.

I squint as I look up because all the rocks are reflecting the heat and glare of the sun. Then I can hardly believe my luck. I'm sure I see someone peering down at me. Yes! He's squatting underneath some overhanging rocks. He must be a Bedouin. Probably looking after goats. Actually, I don't care what he's doing up there. I'm just so glad to see him. For sure, he'll have spare water and then he can take me home to Abudai. This nightmare is about to end. I wave madly at him.

"Hello!" My voice is croaky because my throat is so dry. "I need help."

This red-faced one must be a devil. It is as Old Goat said, after all.

"Go away, you devil! I will kill you if you come up here!"

He yells back at me. I wish he'd speak English. He doesn't seem to want to leave the shade of the rocks. Not that I blame him. I need to get out of the sun as well. It's too hot. I can feel how red my face is.

There's a track that goes along the ridge to where he's crouching, but I'm desperate to get there quickly, so I go straight up even though it's fairly steep. More little rocks slip beneath my feet, and I have to cling onto clumps of dried grass to pull myself up. It's amazing how the thought of drinking cool water has given me that extra strength I need.

"Give me a hand!" I croak, as I'm almost there. This last bit's so steep! I peer up.

I can see the person is a boy, but he looks more Indian than Arabic. I can't tell how old he is. Now he's lying on his stomach peering over the edge at me. He's got the dirtiest face and biggest eyes I've ever seen. His face is small and thin. For a minute, I'm so disappointed I feel like crying. Then I realize that where there's a kid, there must be an adult close by who can drive me to Abudai. Instead of helping me, though, he just stares at me.

"Come on," I say. I feel dizzy again. I hold out my hand. I wish I knew the Arabic for "help me up." But surely he must understand what I want. Maybe he's a sandwich short of a picnic or something and I'm stuck up this slope with a dumbo. He's staring at me like I'm going to eat him or something.

"Looks like I have to do this the hard way, then," I mutter to myself.

As I start to pull myself up, the boy wriggles forward. He sort of half-rises, and I see he's got a rock clutched in his hands and a crazy look in his eyes.

"Allah Akbar! Have mercy on my soul!"

And I need him to take me to his father.

What's the Arabic for "father?" I try to remember, but my head hurts.

Allah the Merciful! Now I see this one is not a devil after all. He is a foreign boy. I am thinking for sure he is going to kill me, but there is a softness in his eyes. Old Goat says all foreigners with their pink skin are soft and weak and cowards. Like girls.

I don't trust him, but we can't stay like this forever. Slowly, but still keeping a hold of him, I get up and pull him to his feet. He stumbles and trips and falls over. The filthy *dishdash* that he's wearing is shucked up to his shins. It's then I see his dirty, bare feet. They're tied together. God! Now I see that his hands, which are no longer clutching the rock, are tied up as well. He's tied up like an animal.

CHAPTER NINE

Just my luck! Here I am, thinking I'm going to be rescued, and it ends up being me doing the rescuing. But what am I going to do now? I try to kid myself that he's been tied up for a joke or something by other kids, but I know that can't be the truth. He looks half starved. And he's filthy, like no one cares about him. But he couldn't have just been dumped. Could he?

I finally remember the word for "father." "*Babu?*" I ask hopefully. He must have a father somewhere. Even if his father's cruel and horrible and treats his kid like this, I'm sure he'll still be happy to take my two hundred dirhams and get me to Abudai.

The kid's whole expression suddenly changes. I'm not sure if he understands.

"I want you to take me to your *babu*," I say loudly. It seems to work, but he speaks too fast for me to understand. I do pick up the words *babu* and *may yet*. And I know *may yet* means "dead." There's an archaeological dig not far from Abudai where an ancient town has been found. The locals call it *Madeenah may yet*—the Dead City.

So I guess he's saying his father is dead. That figures. Well, where's his mother? She obviously doesn't give a toss about him. Maybe she was forced to marry again, and he's got a cruel stepfather or something. I don't really care. Anyone will do as long as they can give me water and get me back to Abudai.

"*Mama?*" I ask him, and my heart drops when I hear him say something about Abudai, and he suddenly looks at me in a hopeful way. I guess that's where he's from, as well. It's true then. He has been dumped. Somebody just wanted to get rid of him for some reason and figured the mountains would be the best spot. He's as lost out here as I am and wants me to help him.

What am I going to do now? I can't leave him tied up; he'll die. But if I let him go, he might try to kill me again. I don't trust him one bit. I half-want to just run away and pretend I never saw him.

For some reason, my gran's face pops into my head. Barby would know what to do. Then, like a coin has dropped into a slot in my head, I have a brilliant idea. I can call her and ask. Get *her* to send help. She's always home. And even if the money runs out she can ring me back. I don't know why I didn't think of it before.

I pull out the phone and my hands are trembling. Please let this plan work. Please have enough battery power.

The battery indicator bar flickers as I key in the number. I can hardly breathe. It rings three times and then there's a click. I hear Barby speaking in a tinny voice and asking me to leave a message. It seems like forever, waiting for the beep.

"Barby, it's me," I yell. "I'm lost in the mountains and I need to talk to you. I need help."

Is he begging his father to forgive him? What terrible deed did this one do to suffer this punishment also? Allah! It seems his father has no mercy.

I hear the kid praying. I am, too. I'm praying that Barby picks up. Sometimes she doesn't get to the phone for a while. The battery bar flickers. Then I get this sinking feeling like there's a rock dropping to the bottom of my stomach. I remember that because we were all meant to be in Melbourne, Barby was going to the city to meet us. We were all going to see Sarah speak on her school's debating team. Barby won't be back at the farm for at least three days, so she won't get my message until then.

The screen goes blank. The battery has died. I shake it, but it's no good. It's dead.

Just like I'll be shortly.

Oh God. Everything's turned out to be such a mess. "Stupid! Stupid! Stupid!" Everyone says I'm really brainy because I can think fast and I have good ideas, but my mum always says I would be smarter if I slowed down and thought about the consequences. Maybe I should have thought this through better.

But how can I think straight when I get mad, like I did this morning? It's like my head's being banged against a wall. And now, here I am, lost in the middle of the mountains with a flat mobile and a charger, but nothing to plug it into.

I know there's nobody to blame but me. I was so mad at Mr. Hartliss. The last thing I wanted to do was ask him for anything. I can almost hear my mum. "Look where that temper's got you now," she'd say.

Lost in the mountains without any water, with some crazy kid who's been tied up like an animal and who tried to kill me. That's where it's got me. And if anybody ever comes looking for us, all they'll find are bleached bones. Maybe they won't even know which one of us is which.

I drop the phone into my backpack alongside my totally useless charger. I guess I can't leave the kid like this, though, all tied up. I pull my Swiss Army knife out of my pocket and open out the blade.

Ah, Allah! Now since this one's father is not showing any mercy, no mercy is he showing me. For sure he is going to slit my throat.

"Stop being such a girl," I say, as I bend down and cut the ropes around his hands and feet, but he's shaking so much it's not easy. Finally I free him, but I don't look into his eyes because I don't want to see that look, like I can help him. I can't. We're going to die and that's that.

The kid's legs must be numb from being tied up. Numb like me. I just sit here and watch him trying to get up, trying to crawl. I don't know where he thinks he can go. There's nowhere to go. Doesn't he realize that?

I feel like crying, but I can't even do that. I'm as dried up inside as this whole scorched country. I lie back on the hot ground, close my eyes, and pull my cap over my face to get some relief from the sun. My head throbs. I can feel all the bites and cuts and scrapes on my arms and legs, but I don't care anymore. About anything.

Then, because my brain won't stop turning things over, I think of something. Even condemned men get a last meal. I remember the After-Dinner Mints.

I sit up, zip open my bag, and find the box. Of course, they've melted, but they're best like that because then you can lick the paper.

I poke my tongue into the wrapping, and even before I taste the bitter sweetness and cool peppermint flavor, the richness of it hits my nose and nearly sends me reeling.

The boy, who's sitting not far away now, rubbing his legs to get them working again, watches me as I lick the mess of brown and green. He looks at me with those big eyes and it's like Tara begging.

"Here," I hold one out to him."You may as well have one, too. We're both goners."

What is this? It cannot be poison for he is eating. But Old Goat says that foreign devils are always taking so why is this one giving? And why is he setting me free?

He stares at me with this strange look on his face.

"You don't have to take it," I say. "I was only being polite."

He snatches the mint out of my hand. I see him

sniff it, then his eyes light up and he pokes his tongue into the paper. Then he stuffs the whole thing in his gob—paper and all. You'd think he'd never eaten chocolate before.

I take time to lick the paper absolutely clean. I'm concentrating so hard on what I'm doing, I don't notice the sky until I realize it's gone dark and it's suddenly got windy. Small bundles of rolling grass race each other across the valley.

I look up, and I'm totally amazed to see shining storm clouds building above the valley. They weren't there ten minutes ago. It's like someone came in when I was concentrating on eating my mint and blew them all up just like big balloons. They've blocked out the sun and it even feels cool now.

For a minute, I stare at them like I've never seen storm clouds before. They're so purple and they shine with a yellow tinge, and they're so fat they bulge downward like someone's belly. Then, like I'm dragging up a memory from a long time ago, I remember: summer storms. Sometimes, sitting up in my room, I've seen the storm clouds piling up over the mountains. Dad told me the name of the clouds, too—cumulonimbus. He said you always know them because they're bumpy and knobbly and look like a huge cauliflower head. I remember my dad saying that if a pilot was silly enough to fly an airplane through clouds like that, the forces inside a thunder-storm could rip the airplane's wings right off.

I hear a crack and there's a flash. Next thing a freezing, wet splodge lands on my head and then I'm drenched.

The kid kneels down and prays as it rains. I'm too busy with my face upward and my mouth open, yelling and drinking.

The rain only lasts a few minutes before the storm passes, but it's like being put through a car wash. One minute a deluge, then the next back into the sunshine. Everything's steaming like it's cooking, and water is running off the rocks and just vanishing into the parched earth. I know what it's like to be that thirsty.

I'm soaking wet. The kid is soaking wet. We're both grinning like mad. He looks like a toothless monkey when he grins like that. I feel light-headed and a bit giddy, like I do after I've snuck one of my dad's beers. But the only thing I've been drinking is the rain. Cool, delicious, soaking rain. It's dripping off my nose and chin like tears, but I'm not crying. Or am I? It's not raining now and yet warm, salty drops are still dripping down my face into my mouth.

Why is this one crying too much? Never am I crying like a *bint*. Not even when I am lost here in this Hell on Earth with this crazy Infidel boy.

CHAPTER TEN
LATE AFTERNOON, DAY ONE

At last, there is some coolness, for the sun is sinking behind the mountains. Soon it will be time for praying to Allah. Five times every day I must be praying and thanking Allah for my blessings. But what blessings are beatings from Breath of Dog and cursings from Old Goat?

Now, maybe, I can be thanking Allah for the blessing of meeting Ad-am because, for sure, this one is quite foolish. I am thinking he is like Shafi the Fool, who also grins too much, since a camel kicked him in the head.

I am sure this must be so, for anything Shafi is having he is giving. Like Ad-am, for in this bag of his he has many clothes and he is giving many things to me. I am especially liking this green head covering, which has pictures of small animals and has two good holes for my ears.

I look at Ad-am and he is grinning too much. Allah! We have nothing to be happy for! I am thinking, maybe, he has not done any bad deed, but has been left out in the mountains because he is crazy.

The valley is in shadow now. I can't see the sun anymore. Not that it's set yet—it's just gone down behind the mountains. It's a relief to think that the most terrible, horrible, frightening day of my whole life is nearly over.

But there'll be another day tomorrow. It'll be just as hot. I'll be just as lost. Am I going to survive that? And what about this kid? The only thing I've really got out of him is that he's called Walid. That just means "boy" in Arabic. It's not a real name, at all.

I wonder why he was dumped out here? Maybe he murdered somebody—just like he tried to kill me. As usual, I keep thinking up more and more dramatic situations. I mean, he doesn't look that bad. In fact, he probably only tried to kill me because he was scared. When I look at him now he makes me grin.

He frowns. Maybe he's worked out that I'm laughing at him.

After the rain we were both soaked and I thought I'd get changed. I've brought too much stuff anyway, so I gave him a spare pair of shorts and a T-shirt and a pair of jocks. He needed new clothes anyway, because his *dishdash* is filthy and it's torn to bits.

He looked at my stuff like he'd never worn anything like that ever before. Because he's so skinny, everything is miles too big. But he did finally manage to work out what to do with the shorts and T-shirt and put them on the right way. Then he insisted on putting the wet *dishdash* back on over everything. But the thing that's cracking me up every time I look at him is that he's put the jocks on his head and pulled them down over his ears. What an idiot!

Before I shove my wet shorts in the backpack, I take everything out of the pockets. I pull out the wad of notes and count them. Two hundred dirhams. They may as well be bits of paper for all the use they are right now.

"Do you know what I could do with two hundred dirhams?" I ask the kid. I know he can't understand a word I'm saying, but I have to talk to somebody or I'll go nuts.

"I could buy ten pizzas or twenty Cokes or a hundred bottles of water."

I stop myself dreaming. There are no shops in the mountains. All I can hope for is that some Bedu will think it's enough money to risk driving to Abudai for.

Ah, Allah! Never have I seen so much money. With

such richness, Mama and I could go home to our country and live like sheikhs.

Suddenly I get a bad feeling. I see the sly way the kid is looking at me. You can see the envy in his eyes. I shouldn't have flashed the money around. It's not like it's a fortune, but he's looking at it like he's never seen this much before. Maybe he can't count and he thinks it's more than it is.

Oh God, what did I have to be so stupid for? Now that he knows I've got money he's likely to bash my head in when I'm asleep and rob me. Maybe that's why he was dumped.

Maybe he was caught robbing somebody. What am I going to do? I can't stay awake twenty-four hours a day.

Hey! I'll just give it all to him. That'll solve the problem. I don't really need the money—I can always give away my mobile in exchange for a ride. Or I can just give them money once I get home because I know Mum keeps a stash in her jewelry box. Or Walid can give them the cash—he wants to get to Abudai as well. My brain is definitely back in gear now.

"Here, take it." I hold out the money.

Walid's eyes nearly pop out of his head as I wave the notes in front of his nose. For a second or two, he just stares, and then he snatches at them and goggles at the money like it's going to go off in his hands.

"Don't spend it all at once."

Allah, this Ad-am is a greater fool even than I first thought. Now I must go quickly to Abudai and find Mama. *Walhumdillah!* Praise Allah for His goodness.

He thanks God but doesn't bother thanking me. Typical! At least he might leave me alone now.

I am having one bad thought. There is no doubt Ad-am will follow me all the way to Abudai, for he is much too foolish to know the way. Allah! Maybe it is even a cunning trick to find his way back to the city. And when we reach there, he may go straight to the policeman and say I am stealing his money. Then I will end up in prison. But I can run fast away. As soon as we reach the city, I will quickly give this one the slip. For now, I will hide these many dirhams under this hat of mine.

"Come, Ad-am. I will show you the way to Abudai."

I've just had a bad thought. Even giving away the money won't get rid of Walid. He knows I'm going to Abudai, and I guess he'll stick with me the whole way. I'll still have to watch my back.

"I don't trust you one bit," I say. "And the sooner we get to Abudai the happier I'll be."

CHAPTER ELEVEN
EARLY EVENING, DAY ONE

"To come to Abudai we must walk in the direction of Mecca, toward the setting sun," I say to Ad-am. "Have you seen how the tall tower turns golden when the sun sinks towards the sea?"

I guess he's asking me what to do now. Why do I have to be the one with all the answers? I turn to get away from that dumb-animal look, and just about go nose to nose with a real animal nibbling on one of the thorny trees nearby. It snickers and trots towards us. It's a goat. A black and brown goat. And it looks as friendly as anything.

"Hey, what do you want, girl?" I ask as I put my hand out. It stops and suddenly looks shy.

"Don't go away." I just want to pat her. I miss Tara, and my mum says I'm good with animals. Sometimes I think, instead of being a pilot, I might study to be a vet like my uncle, and then I could own a dairy farm like Barby's as well.

"Come on, girl." I coax the goat toward me. Of course, she probably hopes I've got some food in my hand. Goats are greedy. When we go camping, sometimes a whole herd of them will come right up to the tents because they think they can get food from us, but Tara always barks and frightens them away. She doesn't like goats.

The goat sniffs my hand and then, slowly, I put my other hand out to rub behind its ears like I do to Tara.

Just then I realize Walid's sneaking up with the rope he was tied up with. He looks like he's up to no good.

"What the hell are you doing?" I yell at him, and startle the goat. It tosses its head and goes into reverse.

"Allah! You fool!"

Walid screeches one of his dumb prayers as he leaps at the goat likes he's in a rodeo and drags it down, holding it by the neck. Then he looks up at me and grins like he's done something fantastic. The goat is bleating its head off.

"Why . . ." I start, as I see the poor thing lying there bleating and kicking the ground. Then I realize something. I was calling it "girl." I was right. It's a she-goat. We can milk it. I even know how to do it, because Barby taught me how to milk cows. A goat can't be that different. But what can I use to put the milk into? I think about the empty bottles in my bag. I can cut the top off them. It's, like, improvising. When I went to Scouts they used to say that although you should always be prepared, there will be times when you're stuck out in the middle of nowhere and you will have to improvise. I used to think it meant improve yourself, but now I know it means to make something up out of other things.

"Hang on to her, Walid," I say, as I tip the bag upside down to get the empty bottles at the bottom. I take my knife out of my pocket and pull out the biggest blade.

This is good. Ad-am understands. He has his knife.

But why does he cut the top off this bottle?

"I will hold the goat while you slit the throat, and then after letting all the blood run out we can make a fire and roast and eat this flesh.

"*La!* No! What is this you are doing?"

I'm squeezing and sliding my fingers, using just the right pressure, so the milk squirts out properly. I manage to get half a bottle.

"Here." I hold it out to Walid. I figure he deserves the first sip, seeing he was the one who caught the goat.

He spits. He's a good spitter. Better even than Jason, who's the best in the Sea Ks.

"Milk is food for babies."

If only I had that blade of Ad-am's, I would soon kill this goat and we would have good food for our journey.

"Okay, if you don't want it, I'll drink it." The milk is warm and slightly sour and salty, but incredibly refreshing.

I feel good that I could milk the goat like I was an expert, and it makes me remember a corny joke: What is an expert? A drip under pressure. I laugh. I must be feeling better about everything. We can keep the goat with us so we'll always have something to drink.

"I'll call you Marge," I say, as I scratch her forehead. It's after Marge Simpson from *The Simpsons*. That's my favorite show.

Marge is quite cute, really (I mean the goat). She's

got big brown eyes and long eyelashes. She snickers just like Marge laughs.

"We'll tie her up to the tree," I say to Walid.

"You must hobble her feet to stop her roaming," I am saying, but Ad-am does not understand.

Walid still seems miffed about something as he points to her hooves. Does he think she's going to kick me or something?

"She didn't even try to kick while I was milking her, so I'm sure she won't now," I say to him, but he doesn't understand me. He shrugs and walks away.

I stay and stroke Marge for a while as I watch her munch happily on some low-hanging leaves.

This one is such a fool to play with the goat. Like a soft girl he is. I feel like giving him a good kicking. Instead, I kick at the ground and I am sorry, for my foot is hitting a heavy tin that has rolled from Ad-am's bag. I sit and hold my foot, which is sore, and I feel even more angry with this foolish boy—he is bigger than me, but he knows no more than a baby.

But what is this tin? I look at it closely, and I am seeing a picture of a dog. Allah! It is true as Old Goat says. The Infidels are unclean. They eat not only the meat of pigs, but also of dogs.

"Unclean!"

I look up when I hear Walid screech. He's holding a tin of dog food. He's probably trying to steal something out of my bag.

"I'll take that, thank you," I say and snatch it off him. The thought that we're going to have to eat Tara's food is enough to make me want to throw up, but I've got to be practical. There's not likely to be much else along the way. I ate all the cheese slices yesterday. And I remember that book I read, about those kids who were in a plane crash in the Andes. They had to eat dead bodies. Chum doesn't sound too bad, really.

I put the tin of dog food back in the bag.

"We need to get started soon," I say, as I sling the backpack over my shoulder. It scrapes against my tight, sunburned skin and makes me wince. I'll be lucky not to come out in blisters. I don't care what Walid wants to do, but I'm not crazy enough to risk walking in that heat again especially now that I haven't got any sunscreen left. We'll travel by night and sleep during the day.

I've got it all worked out. It's like one of those math exercises. If you took 60 minutes to reach B from A, traveling at 120 kilometers per hour, how many kilometers do you need to travel on foot in a day to get from B back to A? I don't know how fast walking speed is, but if we travel about 40 kilometers each night, we could get back in about three nights' walking.

Of course, we've got to get across the desert, but except for the bit with all the orange sand dunes, it's mostly rocks and scrubby trees. I reckon we can do it. I've rollerbladed twenty kilometers in a fun run and that wasn't hard. It only took a couple of hours. All we have to do is double that and we can definitely do it in three days. We'll have one tin of dog food per day and, of course, the goat's milk to drink.

I'm starting to feel like a real explorer.

"We must be moving on, for the journey to Abudai is far," I say to Ad-am.

"Now the sun's gone, we can go, too," I tell Walid. The sky's sort of a silvery grey, but it'll be dark soon. When night comes, it comes quickly in this part of the world. My mum's always complaining that we don't get any long twilights like at home. Here, after the sun goes down, within about five or ten minutes it's completely dark.

And it's so quiet out here it's spooky. Except for a cricket starting up, there's no other noise. In town, you can always hear the air-conditioning systems kick in or the hum of cars in the background, especially where we live, by the main highway. And in our compound you can hear what's going on next door through the walls.

You're never alone there. And even though Mum

doesn't really like compound life, she's happy that even when Dad's away flying, there's always someone around if you need help or company.

All of a sudden, I feel pleased I'm not stuck out here on my own. Even if Walid is a half-wit who can't speak English and Marge is only a goat, at least they're here. It's like now there are others to share this situation with, the whole thing has become more like an adventure than a disaster.

I can't help grinning to myself when I think about what the Hartlisses would have said to each other when they realized I wasn't with Jason's family, that I wasn't in any of the cars. Even better—what are they going to tell Mum and Dad? They'll be feeling pretty stupid, I bet. That definitely cheers me up. And when I turn up safe and sound everyone will be so pleased to see me, they won't even tell me off.

And I'm not even too worried about what'll happen with the war when we get back. Mr. Hartliss reckoned that the Americans would be there before you could blink because they won't want the Mafi controlling the oil wells. When the Yanks arrive with their F-18s and B-52s and cruise missiles, the Mafi won't know what hit them. It'll probably be all over by the time we get back there.

But if we want to get back at all, we'd better get this expedition moving. I look up at the sky. Explorers always use the stars.

"Holy Hell! Where did they all come from?" There are suddenly millions up there, and I can't pick out any stars I know at all. I feel myself starting to panic and I try to remember everything I learned at Scouts. But I didn't go for long because it was down at Ras-al-Haq, which is about an hour's drive from Abudai, and Mum got sick of driving me there every week.

The only thing I can remember is that the North Star is the one to follow, for some reason. But I don't have a clue why or which one is the North Star. How can I tell which direction is north?

Everything's getting blacker. The valley feels like it's closing in around us. We have to get going. We have to walk at least forty kilometers tonight. But which way? I can hardly even see a meter in front of me.

"Which bloody way do we have to go?" I know Walid can't understand a word I say, but I shout at him all the same.

I'm really starting to get angry. Even if he could understand me, he probably wouldn't make a decision anyway. Mr. Hartliss says these people can't make decisions. Not even to save their own lives. He says they reckon it's all in Allah's hands and everything in life only happens because Allah wills it.

"What am I going to do? I'm stuck here in the middle of the mountains with a sneaky little idiot who expects me to know everything and do everything. Why?" I yell at Walid.

He cringes away.

Allah! This one is going mad with the darkness. Maybe now I should be running fast away, for in his craziness he may try to kill me. But without the goat and Ad-am's knife to kill it, I will surely die. What to do?

"It's not fair!" I scream. "It's not fair." And I can't help it. This terrible panicky feeling wells up inside me and I begin to sob in a dry retching sort of way. Why did this have to happen to me? Then, just as I think things can't get any worse, they do.

CHAPTER TWELVE
EVENING, DAY ONE

"The goat!"

Foolish Adam did not hobble its feet and tied this animal only to the tree. It has eaten the rope.

"*Besurah!* Hurry! We must catch the goat."

Walid yells something at me as if it's my fault. But I can't believe she got away. I used double reef knots! Then I realize she's obviously chewed through the ropes. I feel like an idiot. I should have hobbled her feet. Maybe that's what Walid was trying to tell me. Maybe he's smarter than I've given him credit for.

"Look! There she is!" We see Marge through the

trees and we both take off after her. With all the surfing I do, I've got strong legs and I'm a good runner. Walid is, too. He's amazing for someone so skinny. He keeps up with me.

"We've got to catch her," I yell to Walid. I've got this feeling that Marge is our lucky mascot, and if she gets away, then nothing will work out. I can hear her snickering as if she's laughing at us as she trots up the valley. We follow the sound.

We are running fast after the goat. And Ad-am has stopped his crying. Maybe he is not so crazy, but just scared in the darkness. Now, at last, he is showing some sense.

"Together we will catch her."

It's hard to see where we're going and we crash through thorny bushes and trip over rocks. Walid's bare feet must be tough as old boots because he doesn't seem to notice.

Then we hear Marge scrambling up the mountain side. It's alright for her, she's a mountain goat. At least it's not too high or steep. We scramble up after her, then chase her down the other side and up a narrow valley that seems to go for quite a way, deeper into the mountains.

We're both panting and my chest hurts from running so hard.

Then we hear Marge snicker in a way that sounds

like she's pleased with herself. Almost straight away there's another noise. It's a loud splashing.

"Hey!" I shout and turn to Walid. "Good old Marge. She's found water!"

Marge is calmly drinking from a pool of water that's about knee deep on her, so it's up to my shins. She only looks up and bleats a bit as Walid grabs her by the tail and I hold her around the neck. Between us we maneuver her out of the water and get her down on her side. The only thing we've got to tie her up with is my belt. Walid holds her legs together, which is a tough job because she starts to kick. I strap the belt around her legs and make sure it's pulled tight so she can't move. She bleats a bit, and I feel bad, but we can't let her get away again.

"It's okay, girl," I say as she looks up at me with those trusting brown eyes. "We're not going to hurt you. We just want you to come with us and be our pet for the next few days." I scratch the hard part on her head and then the soft spot behind her ears, and she snickers as if she's enjoying it.

Walid and I look at each other and he starts to smile for a change. Out of habit, I swing my arm up and go to give him a high-five like we always do in the Sea Ks.

Walid ducks away like I'm trying to hit him or something.

"What is this? I do not understand. But, if you want a fight, then you must know I am very tough."

He frowns at me. Again.

"Come on, lighten up, Walid. I wasn't trying to hit you. I only wanted to give you a high-five. I mean, what planet are you from? You don't know about high-fives and you wear jocks on your head."

He looks as if he'd like to fight me. I give up. I'm off to jump into the small pool of water Marge has found. It must have been filled by the storm today. I feel all itchy from dried sweat, and I'm hot and sore from my sunburn. Even though it's really dark now, it's still hot, and the water is warm, but it's still nice. It's like being in a bath.

Now Ad-am sees I am too tough so he does not want to fight. But he is so crazy. I do not understand. He cries and then he laughs, he threatens me and then he walks away. Infidels!

This is good to find water, for now I can wash myself before praying. Maybe, when I am clean, Allah will listen to my prayers and help us on our journey to Abudai.

As I lie back in the water, I watch Walid carefully wash his face and hands and feet. Then he faces Mecca, bows and kneels down to pray.

Then I get this urge to do something dumb. I was told once that when Muslims start saying their prayers they're not allowed to stop for anything, not a fire, not an emergency, not for anything. If they do, they think they'll go straight to Hell.

I decide to find out if it's true. I splash Walid. He doesn't move. He keeps muttering his prayers. I splash him again. He still doesn't move. I go for the ultimate test and I stand up and cup some water in my hands and trickle it over his head. He doesn't even shake his head.

I'm starting to feel like an idiot. He really takes this praying business seriously. Our family isn't that religious and we never go to church except for weddings, but I suddenly get this prickling, guilty feeling. What I'm doing would be like shouting in a church and making fun of the priest while he's conducting a service. I've probably really offended him.

He finishes with a last "Allah Akbar" and then lifts his head. His eyes look black and fierce.

"Hey, sorry man, I was just seeing if—" He comes at me, flailing. It's like some crazy switch has been flicked on in his brain. He jumps at me and knocks me backward into the water. Then he leaps on me. It's lucky I'm bigger and stronger or else I'm sure he'd have drowned me. We wrestle, churning the water up. There's water up my nose, in my eyes. We only stop when we're both spluttering and coughing. We're gasping for breath as we back off from each other.

"I really am sorry. I shouldn't have done that. It was a stupid joke." I know I'm gabbling and he can't understand, but I can't help it. He must think I'm a complete moron. He still looks pretty angry. Maybe if I give him something . . . What have I got? What would he want? Then I remember the way he looks at my Swiss Army knife. Like he thought it was magic with the way all the blades and bits pull out. I hate to give it away, but I can always get another one. And if I need it before we get to Abudai, I can always borrow it.

I take it out of my pocket and hold it out. He looks at the knife and then back at me.

"Look, *as-salaam*—peace. Take it. It's yours."

Allah! It is a wonderful thing with so many blades and other things all fitted into a red box. With this I could—

"Now can we be friends?" I search my memory for the Arabic word for "friends". "*Salaak?*" I say, hoping he won't be angry any more.

Salaak? I had friends in my village. Boys I played with. Ad-am is not my friend. And I am thinking: he is an Infidel. Should I be friends with an Infidel? But I think he might be simple; maybe he was wanting only to play. Old

Goat says that Infidels are never praying. And Allah did not strike him down when he was making fun.

Walid looks puzzled. But at least he doesn't look like he wants to kill me any more. I'm trying not to worry about the fact that I've just given him a weapon. But even though he tried to drown me, I think I can kind of understand why. It was just the heat of the moment. For some reason, I'm pretty sure he doesn't really want to do me any harm.

I did not flinch in my prayers, and Allah has rewarded me with this good knife, so maybe it was only a test of my will. If Ad-am wants to play, I will play with him.

Walid smiles at me. I feel so relieved. "Come on, I'll show you how to do a proper high-five."

Walid's a quick learner and soon we're laughing and slapping our hands together like we're old mates. We even go for a swim.

When we finally get out of the water I think about grabbing a dry shirt. It's only then I remember that I've left the backpack in the other valley.

"Oh God! The backpack's got everything in it— the mobile and the food as well as fresh clothes! I didn't even think about it when we took off after Marge."

Walid looks worried too, but it's not about the bag. He puts his hand up to his head and pulls out his wad of dirham notes from under the jocks. They're all wet and screwed up.

"You need to dry them out," I say and reach for them.

He backs away. "I'm not going to pinch your money," I say, as he quickly shoves the soggy notes back under the jocks. He looks at me like he thinks I really was going to steal them.

"I'm more worried about what we're going to eat tomorrow." I mime like I'm eating something.

He is wanting to eat the meat of the dog that he has left in his bag. He probably eats the flesh of pigs as well. Perhaps Old Goat is right. These Infidels are unclean. They do not pray and they do not eat Halal. We cannot be friends.

Walid turns away. Why would he care? He probably hasn't even thought about tomorrow and how we're going to get out of this mess.

In the car Mr. Hartliss said that Muslims never think ahead. He reckons everything is left up to God, then when things go wrong because of something stupid they've done, they can still blame it on Allah. He reckons that will be the Mafi's excuse later on. He said that's the big difference between easterners and westerners. We take responsibility and we make decisions. Maybe Mr. Hartliss was right.

But what do I do now? I try hard not to panic. I've got to think properly for a change and not just rush in. Okay. Do I know where the bag is? All I know is that it's in a valley not that far from here, but I'm not exactly sure how far we came or, for that matter, where we are right now. All I can tell is that this valley has come to a dead end. The cliff face behind the pool of water is steep and would be hard to climb.

The point is, we're already lost. So do we want to get even more lost? Not really. And it's so dark I probably wouldn't even be able to see the bag if I tripped over it. If I'm being smart, I have to admit there's no urgency to go back and get it. The phone is out of charge so no one can ring me anyway.

I'm positive I'll be able to find it when it gets light. I mean, the bag's lime green and Day-Glo orange, so it should stand out amongst all the grey and brown scenery.

Just then my stomach grumbles. I'm starving. I know if I go back now and find my bag, I'll be tempted to eat the dog food, and we've got to save it for when we really need it. I can't even milk Marge because we've got nothing to put the milk into.

I can hear her kicking her legs on the ground and bleating. She's trying to get up. I feel bad about strapping her feet together with my belt, but I can't let our lucky mascot get away again. If I go back looking for my bag now, it'll be too awkward taking Marge and getting Walid to understand. And I'm suddenly feeling so tired. It's been a long day. Too long. And too many things have gone wrong. I just want to curl up and sleep and forget about everything for awhile.

"Ad-am, we must kill the goat for food. This meat is good. Not like the meat of a dog."

I recognize the Arabic word for "dog" and the word, *zain*, which means "good." Yeah." I say, nodding. "*Aywah.* Dogs are good."

A picture of Tara sitting by our gate, hungry and worried, comes into my head. To stop myself thinking about her, I make a new plan for us.

"I know I said we'd travel by night, but there's no point trying to walk a long way if I'm feeling like this. The best thing to do is have a good night's sleep. Find the bag in the morning. Come back here where there's water, eat something and rest up for traveling tomorrow night. Okay?" I point to the sky and sort of mime lying down and closing my eyes.

Walid nods his head. I think he understands.

It's not easy to get comfortable, but I'm so tired I can hardly keep my eyes open. It's been one long day. It feels like a year since Mum came into my room before she left. If only I . . .

I must have finally dozed off. It's the scream that wakes me.

CHAPTER THIRTEEN
DAWN, DAY TWO

I sit bolt upright and realize, by the grey light, that it's around dawn. I feel the hairs on my arms prickling. The sound was so close. It was like someone was being murdered.

I hope it was just Walid having a bad dream. Then I look around and see him leaning over Marge. Even though I feel scared, I almost laugh because he still hasn't taken the jocks off his head. I see Marge kicking her legs. What is he doing? Then I hear a gurgling sound and I breathe in the smell of something so sweet it's sickly. And strong. It makes me cough.

Walid grins at me, and jumps up. He's trying to give

me a high-five like he's done something wonderful.

"Oh God, you've got blood all over your hands!"

"I have killed the goat as we agreed last night, and now we will have a good feast today," I am telling him.

But Ad-am is looking very scared and then, suddenly, he screams at me and starts crying like a *bint* for the life of this goat.

But why? He agreed that we must kill the goat. Because I know he is soft with this animal, I was thinking to kill it before he wakes. Now he is acting crazy.

"That's it!" I scream at him. "You're nothing but a little murderer, and as far as I'm concerned you can look after yourself from now on."

Now I can understand why someone tied him up and dumped him. I feel like slitting his throat. But I can't even touch the knife. Not after what he did with it. It's covered in blood and hair.

All I want to do is get away from him and away from Marge's staring, glazed eyes. She's lying there with her head twisted up at an unnatural angle and that horrible gaping area around her neck like a wide open mouth with blood gushing out.

"Leave me alone!" I scream at him.

I've been running and running and I'm starting to feel sick. And it's too hot to stay angry. It takes too much energy and I need all I've got to climb these ridges. I've decided that after I find my backpack, it'll be best to go back to the pool. There's nothing else to do. I'll need to make sure the water bottle is full before I head off. I don't know when I'll be able to fill it up again. I can't count on storms every day, although I'm hoping some of the *wadis* might have water in them now. Besides, it's too hot to travel for long today and I don't want to end up like I did yesterday. I'm going to try and rest up and do double the kilometers tonight.

I don't care what Walid does. As far as I'm concerned he's on his own—though I bet he tries to follow me anyway. I suppose it's better. At least I can see what he's up to.

I just don't understand. Last night at the pool, I thought we were starting to be friends, but how could I ever trust him now?

"Please let this be the right valley," I pray out loud, as I make my way up the slope. I've done more praying in the last twenty-four hours than I've done for years. God's giving me a hard time, though, because not much is working out. I reach the crest of the slope and look down into the dry, bare valley.

"Please let me see the backpack."

I can see it okay. The orange and green color certainly makes it easy to pick out. But I can't believe where it is.

It's like a bad joke. And the joke's on me, because my bag is not on the ground where I left it. It's in the back of a Toyota truck that's bumping over rocks and swerving around the thorny trees as it speeds out of the valley.

As I watch, it disappears in a cloud of dust.

CHAPTER FOURTEEN
MIDDAY, DAY TWO

"I'm not going to eat Marge. Never!"

I could strangle Walid. He's managed to hack the legs off poor Marge. But even though he's collected a heap of firewood ready to roast them over, he's stuck now because he's got no matches to light the fire.

I almost feel sorry for him. The way he looks disappointed. I think he meant well, even though what he did was so heartless. I just don't know how he could kill a living, breathing, trusting animal like that.

"Let's get rid of the carcass anyway," I say. "It stinks and the flies . . . It's revolting."

We both drag what's left of Marge around the

back of the bushes. At least I don't have to look at her now.

While Walid's sitting by his heap of firewood, playing with the knife I was so stupid as to give to him, I'm thinking about that Toyota truck. People wouldn't be driving through the mountains for no reason. They must have been Bedu. My dad says that Bedu are usually friendly, but you have to be careful not to get on the wrong side of them or say the wrong thing because they can be pretty fierce. He says they live by the rules of the desert, which are pretty much "an eye for an eye and a tooth for a tooth."

I guess they must have been out looking for something, or somebody. Then, like I'm waking up, I realize.

They must have been looking for me. It's been over twenty-four hours now, and my mum would have arrived in Melbourne last night, our time. She and Dad would know by now that I didn't get to Suman and they would have sent somebody to come and look for me.

Now I really hope I am rescued. Except for Marge's raw legs, we've got nothing to eat. All my clever plans are totally blown. Even if I get a major telling off with the certainty of being grounded for years, at least I'll be alive.

And I wouldn't be surprised if the Americans have arrived in Abudai by now and everything's back to normal. Maybe my dad is even at home with Tara right now. Yeah, I bet that's what's happened.

If only there was some way of sending a message telling those Bedu where we are. I try to think how they might have done it in the old days when nobody had phones. Then it hits me. Smoke signals. Of course. But we need to light a fire for that, too. I look at Walid's heap of wood. I'm as stuck as he is.

"If only I could find one small piece of glass. With this, the sun could make a spark in this dried wood."

"What we need is a bit of glass," I say to Walid as he's sitting there flicking out all the little tools on the Swiss Army knife. It's then I see it. We both see it at the same time. The magnifying glass.

We turn and slam our hands together in a high-five.

To get the fire going, we get some dried grass, bunch it together and break up the wood into smaller bits of kindling. Walid carefully holds the glass over the tiny pile. He moves it around until a beam of sunlight falls on it. Underneath the glass it gets really hot, and it doesn't take long before there's a small wisp of smoke. Walid looks at me and grins. I can't help it. I grin, too. In no time, the fire's crackling and the smoke is heading upward in a lovely spiral.

Marge's legs begin to sizzle. I wish that meat didn't

smell so good. My stomach's grumbling and it's starting to feel like it's pressing against my spine. What am I going to eat? I'm going to be too weak to walk anywhere if I don't eat something soon. If only I'd gone back for the backpack last night, then at least I'd have the dog food.

I throw some more dried wood on the fire to get more smoke going. I'll save us both with these smoke signals. I hope those Bedu aren't too far away. Walid's turning Marge's legs over the coals so they don't get too burnt. They're browning nicely.

I'd kill for a plate of chops and peas and mashed potatoes. My mouth begins to water. Chops come from sheep. A sheep would have had to be killed. Marge is dead. I can't bring her back . . .

As I chew on the tough, stringy, half-charred, half-raw meat and suck on the bones, I think about the rest of the journey. Without the dog food, sometime during the next few days maybe I might have had to kill Marge anyway so we could eat. Could I have done it? I'm almost glad Walid has saved me making that decision.

I chuck the bones on the fire and heap more wood on to keep the smoke going. Please, please let someone see it. Then we hear the sound of a truck.

In the distance I can see a swirl of dust in front of a white Toyota. At last, my prayers seem to be answered. It's heading in our direction. Not that I had a chance to have a good look this morning, but it looks like the same one I saw heading out with my backpack.

"Allah! It is Breath of Dog and Old Goat! We must be running fast away. For they are bad men and surely they have returned to kill me."

I hear Walid yell something about a dog again as I jump up and wave my arms in the air and start screaming and running down the valley toward the truck.

It's speeding along, bumping over the rocks heading straight for us. Good old Bedu. They're real country people who notice things like smoke. Not like city people. Barby always says city people are too busy rushing to see important things. Things that could save a person's life. And it's true.

"We're saved! We're saved!" I yell, as I'm dancing around like a lunatic. I feel so fantastically happy, I turn to give Walid the biggest high-five of all time.

But Walid's not there. I look around. He's vanished like he's melted into the rocks.

"Walid, you moron! Where are you? We're saved, Walid!" I yell out, as the truck stops and two men jump out. But they don't look like Bedu. One is tall as a giant and the other is small. The big one has a black beard and a moustache like a black bush sprouting from his face. He's wearing baggy pants and a knee-length shirt like the tribal men from the mountains of Pakistan wear. Tied around his head is a red checked tablecloth. I know it's not really a tablecloth, but my mum's bought one from the *souk*—the market—and she uses it on the barbecue table outside.

The short man is old and skinny and stooped over. He's got an orange beard. It's too orange. It's been dyed with henna. And he's got the biggest nose I've ever seen. He's carrying a long thin stick.

These two definitely don't seem to be the friendly, rescuing types, but then, like my dad says, you can't judge a book by its cover.

But maybe this time you can.

"Where Walid?" Baggy Pants growls at me, as Old Orange Beard limps over and grabs me by the arm. I try to twist away, but he whacks me around the legs sharply with his stick. I yelp. That hurt.

"Where Walid?" Baggy Pants leans down and flecks of spit hit my face. His face is so close to mine, I can see the almost perfect drops of sweat pricking on his wide brown nose.

I suddenly feel something cold clamp around my heart.

These must be the men who tied Walid up and left him for dead.

CHAPTER FIFTEEN
AFTERNOON, DAY TWO

"*Walhumdillah!*"

We all twist around when we hear a blood-curdling scream. Leaping down off the rocks is Walid. He's got the knife in one hand. The blade is out and it winks in the sunlight as he holds it in front of him like a dagger.

"Am I pleased to see you!" I yell at him, and he flashes me a monkey grin and yells something.

"Foolish one! Why did you not run fast away when I am yelling firstly? You are going to get us killed."

"Go, Walid!" Old Orange Beard lets go of my arm and shrieks something at Baggy Pants. Baggy Pants growls and lunges at Walid. I see my chance and put my foot out. Baggy Pants trips and sprawls along the ground, landing heavily with a thud that raises dust.

"Ithnayn walidun Battaa!"

Old Orange Beard screeches something about two boys. I guess he's not happy with either of us. Baggy Pants lumbers to his feet again, shouting.

"Yusalla! When I am getting my gun, I will be shooting! *Allah walidun yamoot!*" I hear Breath of Dog yelling, cursing.

"May you rot in Hell forever," I say to him, as I run.

Walid ducks under Old Orange Beard's long camel stick and slashes and jabs at the tires of the Toyota. There's a hiss of leaking air.

Old Orange Beard hobbles after Walid, screeching at him and trying to beat him with the stick.

But Walid's too quick, twisting and turning this way and that, like he's done this before.

"Come on, Walid!" I scream. "We've got to get out of here."

Walid ignores me and jumps up into the back of the truck where my backpack is.

He grabs the bag as Baggy Pants lunges at him, and chucks the bag at me over his head.

Walid makes a slashing movement and a fine, red line appears down Baggy Pants's arm.

"*Aiee!*"

The big man curses loudly, grabs hold of his wounded arm and dances in a circle.

"Come on, Walid! Let's get out of here." Then I realize, as I look around—we're trapped. We can't go down the valley because it's so narrow at this point and the truck is parked across our only way out. Baggy Pants is at one end of the truck and Orange Beard is at the other.

If Walid had run straight away when I yelled the first time, we might have escaped. It's too late now. But I have to admit it was smart of him to go for the backpack. We'll have my mobile now and some food.

"Come on!" I'm really screaming now and, finally, Walid follows me. The only way to go is up the rocks. We scramble up like goats. But it's then we realize we can only get about halfway. The rest is a straight-up cliff. We'd have to be Spiderman to get up any further.

I'm sort of surprised neither of the men come after us. Sure, Old Orange Beard wouldn't be able to make it, and Baggy Pants has a cut arm, but the wound didn't look that serious.

We're both panting like crazy.

"We must hide, for soon Breath of Dog will bring his gun."

Walid tugs at my arm and I squat down beside him behind a big rock. My head is thumping, and sweat's pouring into my eyes. We're stuck up here on a ledge, behind a rock. It'll be hours until sunset. At least there's some shade, and I've still got my water bottle.

"That was so cool," I say, as we catch our breath. Just then, there's a cracking sound and a high whistle. A rock nearby splits.

"Holy Hell! They're shooting at us. This is not cool!" I'm tempted to peer out from behind the rock, but I know that would be crazy with that madman down there with a gun.

I must be mad myself. I'm in the most dangerous situation I've ever been in, in my whole life, but I feel sort of good. It's got to be all the adrenaline pumping. Why else do I always want to laugh when things are at their most dangerous and frightening?

"We're sitting ducks up here," I say to Walid and grin. He looks worried.

I am thinking I am a big fool. Much more foolish than Ad-am, for now Breath of Dog will kill us for sure. But I was feeling so angry, and I had this good knife, and when I think about the faces of Breath of Dog and Old Goat, when they are seeing the tires go down, I too am laughing with Ad-am.

Walid still looks ridiculous with my jocks on his head, but I have to say he's got a lot of guts. I wouldn't have taken those two guys on with only a pocketknife. Especially knowing they had a gun.

But there are a lot of questions tumbling around my head. I mean, why are they shooting at us? Why do they hate Walid so much? Who are they? Did they really tie him up and leave him to die? He's just a kid. He can't have done anything that wrong. And how did a kid get involved with evil-looking sorts like them in the first place? Was it after his father died? Is one of these men his uncle? I wish I could talk to Walid properly and find out a few answers. From somewhere in the back of my head, I remember the word for "uncle."

"*Aam?*" I ask. Not that it means much because kids here call anyone older than them "uncle" or "auntie." They don't have to be related.

"*La! La!*" No! No! If only Ad-am could understand that this is not a funny business. Soon, we may both be dead.

Just then, I hear a familiar tune from below. It's going "dom diddle domdom domdom." It sounds like the tune on my mobile, but it can't be. I've got my bag, and the battery on my mobile is dead. Fancy those guys having the same tune on their phone.

"I bet they've called for backup," I say to Walid. With a gun and a mobile, no wonder they didn't bother chasing us up the slope. "They must think they can get us any time they like. We can't move without them taking potshots at us, and now there'll be more of them to surround us."

I peer out from behind the rock, carefully, to see what's going on. I can see Old Orange Beard talking on the phone. He's waving one arm around like whoever it is can see him.

There's another crack, and I hear the ping of a bullet ricocheting off another rock a little distance away. Baggy Pants is not a very good shot, or maybe his rifle is old. But I keep my nose in behind the rock all the same.

"Mafi Inglizi. Mafi Inglizi."

We can hear Old Orange Beard yelling. Somebody's got the wrong number, I guess.

Then, over his yelling, I hear the sound of another car.

"This is it. It must be their friends arriving." As I peer out, I see an old dusty Datsun Sunny with tinted windows and big wheels driving at full speed up the valley towards us. It's burbling and roaring like it's got no exhaust. Probably got ripped off ages ago. It's amazing what the locals drive around here, in places where you'd think you could only use a four-wheel drive.

The car pulls up behind the old Toyota truck, which has settled down onto its deflated tires like a hen on a nest. The Sunny's engine is still chugging, all four doors open. There's a blast from the car radio. It sounds like magpies screeching at screaming cats. Well, that's what most Arabic music sounds like to me.

Six guys who look about eighteen years old spring out. All of them are wearing small, round, embroidered caps, so I figure they must be from one of the little villages in the mountains. Maybe they haven't heard about the invasion in Abudai yet. Maybe they won't for another hundred years, either. They're pretty isolated. If we get caught now we could just disappear into these mountains and nobody would ever know what happened to us.

We watch. Baggy Pants and Orange Beard shake hands with the men, and they all talk at once. I can hear them jabbering in Arabic and see them nodding as Orange Beard points to the tires and then up to the rocks where we're hiding.

"This is going to be one big fight. It is best if you take this knife. I will use a sharp rock. We can kill maybe some men before they kill us."

Walid holds out my knife as he picks up a rock in the other hand and grimaces fiercely. He says something about the men, but I don't know what. He can't really think we can take on this lot, can he? That's just plain crazy.

"We can't go up and we can't get down without being caught. Against eight guys there isn't much chance of getting away."

Just then, I notice one of the men glance at the sun, which is now about halfway to the horizon. All of them, including Baggy Pants and Orange Beard, go and wash their hands and face in the pool of water, which is already starting to dry up in the heat.

For a minute, I wonder what they're up to, but when they pull some mats out of the car, I realize it's prayer time. I remember Mrs. Haifa, our Arabic teacher at school, said that the five prayers a day started because people didn't have clocks in the old days. The call to prayer told them what time it was and what everyone had to do.

There's *Fajr*, just before sunrise, telling everyone to wake up, then *Zohr* at midday telling people to finish their morning work. Then there's *Asr* saying get back to work until *Mahgreb* at sunset. The last prayer of the day is *Ishr*. After that everyone's meant to go to bed.

Mum said Christians used to have the same thing in medieval times. They used bells, though, to tell everyone to pray. But when I told Jason that he laughed. He said his dad reckons that kind of thing belongs back in the Dark Ages. His dad says they need to catch up with the rest of the world. "For Christ's sake, it's the twenty-first century," he said.

I'm very thankful for the tradition now though, especially since I'm pretty confident about that business about not stopping prayers once you've started. Not for anything. Not even if someone's getting away . . .

CHAPTER SIXTEEN
MIDAFTERNOON, DAY TWO

"Come on, Walid," I whisper urgently. "This is our big chance. We'll take the car. It's still running." I point to us and the car and to the men kneeling on the ground. I think he understands, but he hesitates.

"But I must pray—I do not want to steal this car instead. Allah will punish us greatly. But if I do not go with Ad-am, the men will certainly kill me. What to do?"

God. I forgot that he probably has to get down and pray too. Isn't there some flextime built into exactly when a Muslim has to start their prayers? When the call to prayer comes from the mosque, it takes most people at least a few minutes to stroll down there, and then they have to wash themselves.

"You can pray in the car. Look, I'll even let you use the rest of this water to wash yourself so you're pure." But I've seen how fanatical he is about his prayers, and I can't take the risk of letting him start so I grab him around the waist and we half-slide down the steep slope, then I half-carry him down off the rocks. He doesn't struggle—I guess he wants to get away as well. He even runs with me to the car.

The engine is still running and the Arabic music is blaring as we jump in. I pull the door shut, and through the tinted side window I can see them all praying. I bet they're trying to finish their prayers as quickly as they can.

"Shut the back doors!" I scream at Walid over the music, as I tug the driver's seat as far forward as I can. My foot still hardly reaches the accelerator pedal.

Walid scrambles over the seat and pulls the back doors shut. I hang on to the steering wheel and peer over the red, velvet-covered dashboard. I'm pleased to see that the car's an automatic because, although Barby lets me drive on the farm and I think I'm pretty good at it, automatics are easier. I shove the gearshift into reverse and put my foot down as hard as I can.

We career backwards, bumping over rocks. I'm not too good in reverse. It's hard to see out the back window anyway, because there's all this gold-fringed stuff hanging all around it, so I'm pleased when we finally get to a place where we can turn. I haul the car around and head off, bumping away over the tracks made by the two cars coming up the valley.

"Allah, the All-Seeing, please forgive Ad-am for this stealing and please keep us in your safety."

"Whoa!" I yell as we hit a hole I hadn't seen and we both fly into the air. That stops Walid's prayers for a moment. When I land back on the seat I shut the magpie music up by pushing the eject button on the cassette player. Now there's only the hissing of static on the radio because that's all you can get out here in the mountains. It's better than the music, though.

I glance in the rearview mirror. The big furry dice hanging from it are swinging like crazy. I can see the men jumping up from their mats. I press my foot down hard on the accelerator again as they come running after us. Old Orange Beard starts hobbling along waving his camel stick. There's a cracking sound and I know Baggy Pants has got his gun out. He misses. Again.

"Keep your head down!" I yell at Walid.

My head's already so low I can hardly see over all the clutter these guys have got on their dashboard.

"Walhumdillah! Wallah, Ad-am!"

I guess Walid's praying again. We probably need all the prayers we can get, and I certainly don't have time to talk to anybody Up There at the moment as I'm too busy hauling this way and that on the steering wheel. I'm not even trying to zigzag to stop Baggy Pants getting a good shot. I'm just having to do it to get around the bushes and big rocks.

We are speeding too fast, like a camel when it is racing. I would like to know how to drive this car like Ad-am, but it looks much harder than riding a camel.

I look down at the speedometer and see that we're doing about 40 kilometers an hour. I want to go faster, but it's too dangerous. The last thing we need now is a crash. So I hang on and try to avoid the rocks and the bushes and the holes. This car hasn't got a lot of clearance. We could easily rip off the oil sump or puncture the petrol tank. At least I don't have to worry about the exhaust.

Allah be praised! There is a big bend in the valley and the road along the *wadi* is looking much more smooth.

Before we take the bend and follow the old

riverbed where the rocks are not so big and there aren't so many bushes, I quickly glance in my rearview mirror again. Some of the men are still chasing us, but they're eating our dust.

I'm almost starting to enjoy myself as we career along the *wadi*. It's wider and smoother here. I like driving, and Dad has even told me that's part of the reason why I'd be a good pilot like him. The best thing now, though, is the air-conditioning. The car might be old, but the a.c. is a good one. It's blasting out freezing air into our hot, sweaty faces. It's like heaven on a stick—my mum is always saying that.

But the whole car smells like an ashtray.

That's when I remember my mobile.

Brilliant! I can charge it up using the lighter in the car.

"Bag!" I say to Walid, as I glance down at the backpack at his feet.

As I do, I see a movement—something black with lots of legs, crawling out of one of the side pockets. Just a spider. Must have got in there when it was in the back of that old truck. It was full of hay and other stuff.

The spider scuttles under the seat. I'm not scared of stupid spiders. Not even big ones. I grin a bit, though, when I think what my sister would do if she were here. She'd probably be screaming her head off by now.

No time to worry about spiders. I don't know the word for "mobile" in Arabic, and I couldn't explain about charging it anyway, so it's easier to just look for it myself. I drive for a while, until I figure we've been traveling for at least half an hour. We're definitely far enough away from the men to pull over, so I put my foot on the brake and ram the gear into park. After we skid to a halt, I grab the backpack and rummage through it. It smells a bit off with all the damp gear in there.

"Where the hell is my mobile?" I upend the bag. The car starts to look like my bedroom. Jocks and socks and T-shirts and shorts are everywhere. A tin of dog food rolls out into Walid's lap. He picks it up, looks at it, then drops it quickly, like it's dirty.

I don't know what his problem is. I mean, I know the Arabs hate dogs, but he's always talking about them. Maybe he was cursing. The worst thing a Muslim can say to someone is that they're the son of a dog.

"*Kalb zain*—dogs good," I say. "Wait until you meet Tara, then you'll know how *zain* dogs are." It won't be long until we're back home, at this rate. But I'd like to charge up the mobile so I can make a few calls and let everyone know I'm okay.

I find the box of After-Dinner Mints. It's a bit squashed. Walid's eyes light up. "We deserve it," I say, as I hand him one and stuff one into my own mouth.

"But where's my mobile?" I look through all the pockets on the outside. It isn't there. Neither is the charger. It couldn't have fallen out.

"Holy Hell," I say, as I finally figure out what must have happened. "Old Orange Beard must have pinched it when he and Baggy Pants found my backpack. And he's probably charged it up in the Toyota."

I think back to when Orange Beard was talking on the phone. From what he was saying, it was obvious he was talking to somebody who was speaking English.

"It had to be Barby. Or my mum or dad," I tell Walid. "That's what they'd do. They'd call me as soon as they found out I wasn't with the Hartlisses or when they got my messages."

I think about all the desperate messages I left on their voice mails, when I was lost. They must be pretty worried.

"Ad-am we must go fast away again or maybe the men will come to catch us."

I think Walid is trying to tell me to pull myself together. He's right.

"What the hell. There's nothing I can do about it now and I'm certainly not going to wait here for that lot behind to catch up. What would I do? Ask for my phone back? Anyway," I say, as I put the gearshift back into drive and we lurch forward, "I suppose we're heaps better off having a car than a phone."

I look across at Walid and grin at him. "Don't look so worried. We'll be okay. All we have to do is find a road and some signposts." I keep talking, trying not to chuck a tantrum like I normally do. It feels good being this calm. Maybe losing my temper isn't such a good thing. I can never think of anything except what's upsetting me and I usually end up in even more trouble.

"I'm still not sure where we are, but we can't be far from a proper road." I quickly glance at my watch. It's nearly 5:30 pm. "As long as we can find a road and a signpost before it gets dark we might be home in less than two hours." The thought of home like it always was—with Mum and Dad and Tara and even Sarah—makes me want to be there. Safe.

"Everything will be back to normal for sure." If I tell myself that enough, maybe it will be true. Anyway, where else can I go? Suman's too far away and I don't know anybody there.

It's then I check the petrol gauge. It's less than a quarter full. "Damn!"

I can feel the panic start, but try to squash the bad thoughts and come up with another solution straight away. We've got plenty of money. With the two hundred dirhams I gave Walid, we can fill the car up and even get something to eat. Lots of Arabic kids my age drive cars, so the attendants probably won't even care. Look how much they cared when they saw me on my own yesterday.

We drive on down the wadi. But, after awhile, I realize the sides of the valley are less steep than they were. Then we finally come around another bend. Suddenly it looks like we've driven to another planet because the scene in front of us is totally different.

There's a wide, flat graveled area that must have been a huge river thousands of years ago, but it's completely dried up now. On the other side of this huge *wadi*, away to the horizon, are seas of orange sand dunes.

All the way along the *wadi* are Bedu camps. I can see the rusty tin sheds and the crooked fence posts, the colored doors, the old rotting blankets used to make walls and roofs for the sheds and yards.

The camps look untidy against the smooth, brightly colored dunes. There are pieces of rubbish scattered around, and blue plastic bags hanging in the few scraggly trees. I can't see any sign of people. They're usually deserted because, although the Bedu keep their goats and camels at their camps, nobody lives there. My mum says almost all the Bedu live in towns now.

I pull up. I've got no idea where to go from here. And I have to go to the toilet as well by now. That'll give me an excuse to stop and to think straight at least.

"We're lost," I say to Walid. "I don't know which way it is to Abudai from here."

"We must be traveling over this desert in the direction of the setting sun to be finding Abudai."

I wish my Arabic was better so I could understand exactly what Walid was saying, but I guess he said something about the desert.

"Yeah," I say, "I wouldn't want to be trying to get across that."

The one thing I do know is that we're on the edge of what's called the Empty Quarter. And that means empty. There's nothing there except sand and more sand. I suppose there are one or two oases in there somewhere, but you'd have to be lucky to find one.

Despite our predicament, I still feel reasonably cheerful now as I hop out of the car. After the air-conditioned comfort of the car, the heat blasts me. At least it's cooling down a bit now, with it being late afternoon. Walid gets out as well and squats—he watches me like I'm a loony as I pee standing up. He points to the sun. It's glowing a light yellow and sitting right on top of the haze above the desert.

"We are needing to be heading towards Mecca," I say again to Ad-am, and this time I am pointing so he is knowing.

"Yeah, yeah," I say, "I know the sun is going to be setting soon and then it'll be time for your prayers. Again."

I like watching the sun set. I'm always on the look out for the green flash, which is meant to happen just after the sun sets. In Abudai, it's sort of nice watching the sun, red as flames, sit on the sea for a minute or so, then slowly sink down into it like it's putting its fire out for the night. And in the summer, after the burning heat of the day, it's always good to see the last of it for about eight hours.

"Maybe you can ask Allah which way to go," I say, and then I realize that in a funny way He might already have shown us the right direction. Walid's still looking at me and pointing like he's really trying to tell me something and now, finally, I realize what it is.

Muslims pray facing the setting sun. The sun sets in the west, and in Abudai the sun sets over the sea. So that means by traveling in the direction the sun goes down, we'll be headed straight for the coast. Once we hit the coastline it'll be easy to find Abudai. And then all I have to do is go back to our house and wait for Mum and Dad to get back. If Dad's not back already.

"Brilliant!" I say to Walid, "but we can't go over the desert. Even in a four-wheel drive we'd get bogged, because the sand is so fine. We'd have no hope in this thing. So what do you think we should do now?" I really want his advice. I wish he could speak English because he seems to be a lot smarter than me about these things.

"We've got to work this out quickly," I say. I look around to get my bearings. I need to know which direction is north and which is south. I remember that some nights on the beach after sunset my mum likes to point out the Big Dipper, which I know is in the north.

I turn towards the setting sun and I close my eyes. I try to imagine being down on the beach. Now, which direction does she always point in? I remember that it's hard to see because of the lights of Abudai.

"Can you help me here, Walid?" I point to the west. "This is . . ." I search through my head for the Arabic for west.

"*El-gharb,*" Walid says suddenly and grins.

"Yeah, yeah—*el-gharb,* west. That's great. Now if I'm facing west as if I'm looking at the sea, then the—*shamaal*—north—would be to the right of me." I hold out my arms and point north.

"Aywah". Walid says. That means "yes."

"So that means my left arm is pointing down the *wadi* and that must be—*janoob,* south. The mountains behind are in the east—*esh sharg.*" I feel more pleased with myself than I would if I'd got an A in English.

It's like we've worked this out together. We turn and do a high-five. We're a pretty smart team.

Then I look up at the sky because I remember even that's got a direction. It's called the zenith. That's the highest point. And directly below me, the lowest point you can go is the nadir. It's then I get this really weird feeling as we're standing here, in the middle of nowhere, in this huge dried-up *wadi*. I feel as if Walid and I are standing right on the spot where north meets south and east meets west. There must be such a spot. Right?

"*Yallah!* Hurry! We must go—soon it will be dark."

Walid brings me back to my senses.

"Yeah, we'd better go."

We jump back into the car and set off toward the north. Somewhere there's got to be a road off here to Abudai.

The *wadi* stretches to the horizon and it's wide and straight enough to be a racing track. With the great excuse of having to hurry to find a road before the sun sets, I get this sudden urge to floor it. So I do, and we hurtle along faster and faster. The needle reaches seventy, then seventy-five, and then flickers to eighty. The gravel rattles underneath the floor of the car and clouds of dust rise behind us. This is amazing fun. I quickly glance over at Walid to grin at him.

Then Walid yelps and grabs at his neck.

And I see the spider.

I let out a shriek that my sister the drama queen would be proud of. It's black and hairy with huge pincers, and it's scuttling down Walid's shoulder. Now I recognize it. I've never seen a real one before, but I've seen pictures of them.

It's a camel spider. But it's not the spider that scares me. It's the bright red blood trickling through Walid's fingers.

I stamp my foot on the brake and we begin to skid.

CHAPTER SEVENTEEN
EARLY EVENING, DAY TWO

I clamber out of the wreckage. I'm shaking like mad and choking on the orange dust in the air. I still can't believe how quickly the car rolled. It's landed back on its tires, but the windscreen is shattered and the top is pushed in. Right now, I'm glad I'm a shorty. If I'd been much taller, I would have been crushed for sure.

Then I see Walid. He's all crumpled up on the back seat. He didn't have his seatbelt on and he must have been thrown around when we rolled. I drag him out. He looks even skinnier and smaller than usual. His head seems too big for his body and his eyes are closed.

"Are you okay, man?" He doesn't move. "Oh God, don't let him be dead!" I pray, and shake him. He moans.

"Thank God, thank God." He's alive, but he still doesn't look good.

I know it's not from the bite of the camel spider. They're not poisonous, but they have big fangs and if they're frightened they do bite. I can see the marks where it's punctured his skin. But where is it now? Suddenly there's a movement to my left and it scuttles out from underneath Walid and heads off across the rocks.

"That's for giving me such a fright and for making me crash and . . . and for hurting Walid." I stamp on it. Hard. It helps stop me shaking.

I turn back to Walid. I've got to do something. He's got a big bump on his head and he's still out of it. I find a sock in the car and use some of our precious water to mop his face. There's no point trying to clean it.

The next thing is to get the hell out of here. If those men catch us now, we'll be history.

My skin prickles when I remember what Dad said about an eye for an eye and a tooth for a tooth. We've just wrecked their car. What does that count for?

I can't believe how cool-headed I'm being, despite the situation. Not panicking at all anymore. They say it happens sometimes when you're in a real emergency, like after an accident—somehow the stress helps you think more clearly.

As much as I don't want to move Walid again, I know I've got to take the chance and hope that he hasn't broken any bones and isn't bleeding inside. I squat down and haul him up on my back. Luckily, with all the surfing I do, I'm pretty strong, and he's unbelievably light. But I can't carry the backpack at the same time. Anyway, everything in it is scattered all over the place.

"I'll just have to get you into a hiding place first and then come back for anything important."

I look around. The only place to hide out now is in one of the Bedu camps. But once they find the wrecked car they'll be sure to search them. We've got no choice, though. At least there are lots of camps, and if we head for the one furthest away, that should be the last place they'll look.

I start to trudge back down the *wadi*, with Walid bumping on my back. A little voice in the back of my head is yelling at me, calling me an idiot. "Think where you'd be if you hadn't been so dumb!" But I'm not listening, because if I do, then all the panic inside will rise up and blow the top of my head off.

As I see the sun slowly lowering itself into the haze, I can hardly believe it's only been about fifteen minutes since we were looking at it before. I

wish it was dark already. Then there'd be less chance
of them seeing us. They might even miss the car in
the dark because it ended up on the other side of a
sand dune.

Then Walid wakes up. He mutters like he's not
properly with it. At least he's still alive.

"*La! Ana as if. Ana as if, Shirin.*"

"It's okay. I know you're sorry, but it wasn't your
fault. It was mine." He probably can't hear me, but I
feel so bad that he's been hurt because of me being
stupid.

By the time I reach the furthest Bedu camp,
Walid is still muttering and whimpering and he feels
like he weighs about ten tons. My back and legs are
aching, but I try not to hurt him when I put him
down onto a pile of cut grass inside a small shed
made of rusty tin and dried palm fronds. There's an
old carpet on the ground that's so dirty it's impossible
to pick out the pattern.

"There is too much jolting. This camel is too slow. I am
never winning on this camel, no matter how much I am
beating and beating with my camel stick. *Aiee!* The camel
stumbles. It is not a camel. It is I that is being beaten.

Allah! One hundred curses on that Breath of Dog and
Old Goat, for once again they are beating with their
sticks. I am feeling the pain all over my body and this
blackness is spreading . . .

Walid moans a bit as I spread a sack over him. If they do come in here and it's dark, and they only glance in, then they might not notice him. Of course, that's if he doesn't move. I wish I didn't have to go. But as much as I'd like to just lie down in the hay and get my breath back, I know I've got to get those supplies. We need water and food. My belly is grumbling. Chum is starting to sound delicious.

"I won't be long."

"Allah, where am I?" I am having nightmares of being in Hell."

I smell camel dung and dried grass and I hear camels munching and moaning and stamping their feet. But as my eyes are opening, I do not see Badir and Mustapha who always sleep together on the ground near to me.

Too much my head is hurting. Am I falling from a camel in a big race? Or has Breath of Dog given me one tremendous beating? Then I am remembering Shirin. Her screaming and her blood. And the shootings and Breath of Dog and Old Goat taking me to this Hell on Earth where there is only hotness and darkness . . . and Ad-am.

Slowly, as the confusion is going from my head, I remember all things. I look around, but I do not see my friend.

I call and call, but he is not here. He has gone. Like Babu and Mama. Like Shirin. Always everyone is leaving.

Inside my belly is an emptiness, and I feel the tears coming into my eyes.

"Allah, may You curse this stinking soul of Ad-am who said he was my friend but who is nothing but an Infidel and an Unbeliever. And may You curse me too as one big fool for thinking he is not treacherous like all foreigners. Maybe while I was sleeping he has robbed me.

Quickly, I look for my dirhams. He has not taken them. Why not? I do not understand. And why do I not feel happiness any more, even as I look at all these dirhams?

"Hey, man, are you okay?"

Along with my gear and a few other essentials, I found a torch in the car and I shine it around the shed looking for Walid. He's sitting up in the corner.

He's got all his grubby dirham notes in his hands, but he's not looking at them in the same way he did before.

In fact, he's not really looking at them at all. He's just staring at nothing. And he's crying.

I didn't think he could cry.

"Ad-am! *Walhumdillaah!*"

"Hey. It's cool, Walid. It's cool."

Walid leaps up when he sees me. He's still crying, but he's grinning madly, too, and then he gives me a big high-five. I'm relieved. He's not badly hurt after all. Probably has a few bruises, but it's hard to tell under all that dirt. He must have a terrible headache, though, and I'd say his neck would hurt from that bite.

"I found some more water in the car," I say quickly, as I show him four bottles of springwater that had been under the seat. "And look," I say, ripping the lid off a tin of Chum. "I've even brought us something to eat."

He looks at me in horror.

"I'm not that fussed on eating it, either," I say, "but I'm starving." The smell of the meat, which is meant to be chicken, almost puts me off. But the worst thing is that it makes me think of Tara. Here I am, about to eat her food, and she probably hasn't had anything to eat for days. I can picture her sitting there, by the gate of our compound, not moving, waiting for us to come home. She won't leave that spot unless—

"*Kalb mu zain,*" Walid says, looking totally disgusted.

I start to feel angry. There he is again. Going on about dogs. Poor Tara's starving, and he's not only turning his nose up at her food, but he's saying dogs are bad.

"*Kalb zain!* Dogs good!" I almost scream at him. "My Tara is the best dog in the whole world." The

Arabic words pop into my head. *"Tara kalbi zain.* The *zain*est. *Zain*er than most people I know."

'You are an Infidel to eat dogs—*yaakul kalb.* I am never eating the meat of dogs."

"Yaakul!" He said *"yaakul kalb!"* That means "eat dog!" "Do you think I would eat my dog?" I stare at him in horror.

He points to the picture of the dog on the tin, and I realize what he must have been thinking. And as we stare at each other, I also realize we're having an argument and we don't even speak the same language.

"No, *la kalb.*" I shake my head. I don't know how to explain that it's meat for a dog and not meat of a dog and, by now, I'm too hungry to care.

"If you want some you're welcome to help yourself. But we're going to have to use our fingers."

I dig in. As I bring a lump of the meat up to my mouth, I suddenly smell it and nearly gag, but I force myself to shove it in and swallow it as fast as I can without letting it sit in my mouth too long. It's salty and sort of wobbles down my throat like jelly.

"It's not bad, really," I say to Walid, as I offer him the can, then lick my fingers.

Ad-am is saying it is not dog, and I am very hungry.

He hesitates for a millisecond, then takes some, too.

As we share the meat, I try not to think about the words on the tin that say "not for human consumption." We finish off with an After-Dinner Mint, to get rid of the taste. Walid really loves them. I show him how to take the paper off and how to suck it so you get the most out of it. I even teach him how to say "chocolate."

Then, while we're talking, I try to explain to him about Tara and how I'm going back to rescue her. I think he gets it.

"And to think we might have been home by now and I'd be able to let her into the house." I have to try not to think about "if onlys."

I am understanding now that Ad-am has a dog he calls Tara. The way he looks when he says her name is like how I felt for Shirin. I tell Ad-am all about my Shirin. Even though I know he will not understand.

Walid talks about a sweet camel, but he talks too fast and I can't catch any of the other words.

What are we going to do now? I do have to think about that. After what we've been through today, I'd love to just lie down and sleep, but I'm nervous—scared that we will be caught by those men who are after our blood. It won't be long until they're on our tails again.

Then, as if because I was expecting it, I see a pin-prick of light through a crack in the palm-frond wall.

"There's a car coming up the *wadi!* It's heading this way." Of course, we don't know who it is, but suddenly the walls of our hiding place seem way too flimsy.

"We'll get caught for sure. What'll we do now?"

CHAPTER EIGHTEEN
EVENING, DAY TWO

"*Jemaal!*" Walid shouts, and I know this means camels.

"Yes! Brilliant idea, Walid." We race out to the yards at the back of the hut, and I realize it is a brilliant idea, except for the fact that I've never actually ridden a camel before.

This should be interesting.

Then Walid suddenly stops and looks dead scared and starts muttering to himself. For the hundredth time, I wish I knew more Arabic. There's something wrong, but I don't know what. And we don't have time for this.

"Come on!" I shout at Walid. He's standing there shivering, like he's cold or scared or something. I've never seen him look this scared before, not even when I first found him, all tied up. What a time to start acting like a wuss.

"Come on! We've got to get going. The car's heading this way, and if we get caught . . ." I don't even want to think about it. I pull open the rusty old gate.

"Here, girl," I call out to one of the camels, but it moves as quickly as it can away from me, followed by the other one. I don't want to scare them, but I'm so scared myself. I run after them. They kick their back heels at me. God, I'm never going to catch either of them. And I can see the lights of the car getting closer.

"Walid, you've got to help me. Between us we can corner them."

The death of Shirin has come before my eyes as if it is happening once again. I can hear her screaming in painfulness. It has suddenly made me very much afraid of ever touching a camel again.

But then, Ad-am calls, and this breaks the spell cast upon me.

Foolish one! He is frightening the camels.

"Ad-am, do not run. You must call to them—softly, in this way—Ahh Krrrr Krrrr, tall ones. All is well. Kirrip! Kirrip!"

The camels stop and look at Walid.

Walid's making a sound like a cricket rubbing its wings. But it must be like an abracadabra word for camels, because slowly, one of them moves towards him. Walid holds out his hand and makes a sort of guttural clicking noise in his throat. He reaches up and pats its neck.

"Kirrip Kirrip." I am looking into the eyes of this one. They are soft, like ripened dates. She is like my Shirin.

And she is grumbling like Shirin. With my hands touching the roughness of her neck, the fearfulness inside me is going, slipping away like the night shadows at dawn.

The camel mutters and growls. She lowers her head as Walid pulls on her tufty mane. He knows. He knows how to handle camels and he doesn't look scared at all.

It's amazing. He's getting the camel to do exactly what he wants. She's grumbling and moaning, but she kneels down in the awkward way camels do, lurching first one way then the other.

"Ad-am! *Tafiaal henaa!*"

I think Walid's telling me to climb on. Oh God.

"Do you really expect me to get on this thing?" Maybe this is crazy after all. How am I going to ride it? I don't even like riding horses.

Why is he stopping? Is he afraid of riding a camel?

"This one will be slow for she is older. *Yallah! Yallah!*"

The headlights of the car are getting closer. I know I have to get on.

"But where do I sit?" I can't sit in front of the hump on the camel's neck and the rump just slopes away. I'll slide off.

"Henaa! Henaa! You must sit here."

Walid is pointing to the spot behind the hump. But how can anyone ride a camel without falling off backwards?

Walid helps me up onto the camel's back. I feel out of balance with the backpack on and nearly tip off backward.

He makes signs to show me that he can carry the bag for me.

"Great." I hand it down to him. He hoists it onto his back, then slaps my camel lightly on the rump and hands me the rope that's part of a halter around the camel's head. As I grab hold of it, the camel lurches up onto its hind legs. I almost fall off frontward this time.

"Whoa!" This is like being up on a wave. Automatically I lean my body away from the movement as we sway first to one side, then the other as the camel finally gets up on all four of its long skinny legs.

"Now what do I do?"

"Erkab! Ride! Go toward the dunes. The car will not be able to follow."

He yells something at me, but I'm so busy trying to ride this thing and not fall off that I can't concentrate on what he's trying to tell me.

While I'm getting used to being up on the camel, Walid's already mounted and his camel is ready to go. He looks comfortable. Like he's ridden camels hundreds of times before. He probably has. It makes me wonder—

"Yallah! Let's go! If these men catch us stealing these camels the punishment will be very great. We must get fast away."

"We'd better get out of here fast!" I'm starting to really panic now because the lights of the car are getting very close. If they hadn't seen us before, they've got a good view of us now. It's like being in the beam of a searchlight. I shield my eyes and kick the camel hard.

"Yaiee!"

Walid shouts and slaps my camel on the rump,

this time with a long stick that's he picked up from somewhere. I nearly fall off backward as we lurch forward toward the large sand dunes that rise up behind the camp; they're the size of small hills.

We take off at a gait that's not a trot and not a gallop. It's fast and it makes me bump up and down and roll from side to side as if I'm on a boat in choppy seas. It's an unbelievably rough ride, but Walid seems okay. He's upright and pumping with his arms like he's marching. He's not bumping up and down like I am.

This Ad-am is a bad *rakeeba*. He is like a sack of rice riding on his camel. Ah, Allah, please do not let him fall.

Behind us, I hear a man shouting. Quickly, I look over my shoulder. In the lights from the car, I can see it's not Baggy Pants or Old Orange Beard or even any of the men in the old Sunny. It's a Bedu man. He must have just come out to feed his camels and goats after the heat of the day was over. He has a black beard and waves his fist fiercely at us. Then he jumps back into his Nissan SUV and comes speeding after us.

"Come on, girl!" I urge my camel to go faster, and I lean as far forward as I can. The hump sticks into my stomach, but I keep a tight hold on that tufty mane and try not to be mesmerized by the camel's neck, which sways and bobs like a big snake being charmed by music.

No point stopping now and trying to explain why we're stealing his camels. From the look on that man's face, I've got a feeling he wouldn't understand. I go cold when I remember the punishment for stealing, according to Islamic law—the right hand is chopped off at the wrist.

"Come on, girl!"

The car revs hard as it charges up the dune after us. We race up the soft sandy slope, with me hanging on grimly.

I hear the car revving. Too hard.

I glance behind again. Sand is spraying out from the rear wheels of the car. It's not going anywhere. It's bogged.

As we race over the crest of the dune and down the other side, Walid looks across at me and grins his monkey grin.

CHAPTER NINETEEN
DAWN, DAY THREE

"I'm positive that glow along the horizon ahead is Abudai," I say to Walid.

But I'm not positive at all. There's something not right about it.

But it has to be. There aren't any other towns that big along the coast that'd make the nighttime look like it's turning into day.

Walid frowns and doesn't look too excited. I have to say I'm almost too tired to care. After the longest day of my life, I've now had the longest night. I never thought there could be anything more boring or more uncomfortable than a night flight from

Abudai to Melbourne. Now I know there is: riding Humphreda all night.

I've called my camel Humphreda for two reasons. One is the obvious—her hump—and the other is because she sounds like she's always in a humph—moaning and groaning all the time. Especially when it comes to going up sand dunes. I have to keep kicking her to make her go. With her hump jutting into my stomach, I can't sleep, but I'm so tired I can't stay awake, either. And I've even got motion sickness from all the swaying.

Then to my amazement, all of a sudden, she starts to trot. Up a dune. I get such a shock I nearly fall off backward. I hold on hard as she trots faster still. I can't believe she finally wants to catch up with Walid. After traveling the whole night at the slowest plodding pace she could manage without actually stopping, this is truly incredible.

"Allah! What fools we have been!"

I hear Walid curse. I can't see what's so bad about the fact that my camel has finally decided to get a move on. Then, as we near the crest of the dune, I realize the glow has grown. In the grey, early dawn light we can see a jagged outline on the horizon.

"I can't believe it!"

But it's true. I haul back on Humphreda to stop

her charging down the other side of the dune. It's then that we see the rim of the orange-red sun slide up behind the mountains ahead of us. Below is the wide *wadi* and the Bedu camps.

"But that can't be right."

I wish the sun was wrong. But I know it's us. Somehow we've traveled in a circle. A full circle. Instead of looking at the coastline, we've been heading back to the mountains.

"How could this have happened?" I look over at Walid. He looks as brain-numbed and tired as me. And just as stupefied. He shakes his head and mutters.

"Allah, curse me. Fool for not knowing these camels would follow their noses back to their home where there is water and food."

Deep down I know how it's happened. It's because I've never really had to pay attention to how nature works. I thought we could just look up and follow a star. Everyone says you can navigate by the stars. But I didn't really understand that the stars move in the sky. I've never had to think about it.

When I looked up through the night, I just thought the stars were in different positions because we were moving and I was looking at them from a different angle. And there are so many stars up there. It's easy to mistake one for another.

But it wasn't that. We were on a rotating Earth following a moving star.

"What an idiot I am," I say to Walid. All that long night wasted going in a circle.

I'm tempted to head back to the Bedu huts and wait out the day, but what if that man's still there? Or Baggy Pants? Or the mountain villagers?

I try to haul Humphreda around, but she absolutely refuses to move. I kick her. She sways her neck around and shows me her yellow teeth, but still won't put one foot in front of the other.

"What's wrong with this camel?"

"*Maaye. Jamaal awiz maaye.*"

Walid says something to me, and then takes off down the dune. Toward the Bedu camp.

"Hey! Where are you going? We can't go that way. We'll get caught." He doesn't take any notice. "Are you just giving up?"

I can't believe Walid wants to give up. Not now. Not after everything we've been through. I know it's not going to be easy traveling through the desert in the heat of the day, but we've got the camels and we've got plenty of water. But he seems determined to go back to the camp. I can't let him get caught by himself.

"Okay, Humphreda, you're going home." I don't need to kick her. She takes off at a trot, down the dune. I pray that there's no one around. At least I can't see the car.

All is quiet and still. But what if they're hiding? Waiting for us. I'm so scared I want to slip off Humphreda and run off into the desert, but I can't let Walid face the danger on his own.

When I ride into the yard after Walid, it does seem deserted.

Walid has slid off the back of his camel and is letting it drink deeply from a water trough. Humphreda trots over and puts her snout in as well, snuffing up the water.

"*Jamaal awiz maaye. Ba'd ehnaa ruh!*" he says.

"The camels need water to travel so far in the desert. Without it they too will die.

"Don't you know this, Ad-am?"

Walid points at the water trough and then back towards the desert. I finally realize that he's only come back to let the camels have a drink.

"But they're camels. I thought they could go without water for days."

He shakes his head as if I'm an idiot and lets the camels take their time drinking. The one good thing is that with all the adrenaline pumping through me, I'm ready to get going again. As soon as possible. I'm hardly feeling tired at all. We fill up the eight empty bottles with water—four each. The water is slimy because it's from the trough, but it's water and we'll need every drop we can get.

"We'll put them in the backpack, but it'll be too heavy for you to carry," I say to Walid. "I'll strap it to Humphreda's neck in front of me." After being without water on that first day, I feel better if I've got plenty of it close and handy.

I squint towards the sun. It's white hot already, and a haze is forming over the mountains. It's going to be hellish in the desert, but what else can we do?

At least I've got the navigation figured out now. We'll have to travel by day, because if we keep the sun behind us in the morning and then in front of us in the afternoon we'll always be heading west.

One good thing is that after her long drink, Humphreda seems happier as we set off again. Up and over the dune, we plod off into the Empty Quarter. Again.

God, I hope we come across one of those oases or else we'll be goners.

Allah, it is hot! This is truly a Hell on Earth. It is a good thing Ad-am took out some of his clothes from the bag, for these I have draped around my head to save myself from the burning sun. But Ad-am is crazy, for he is throwing off his clothes.

"You must wrap something around your head to stop the fierce sun from sending you even more crazy," I say to Ad-am.

"It's too hot to put on more clothes." I guess Walid is trying to tell me to cover up. He's worse than my mum.

By 10:00 a.m. the day is shimmering. It's so hot the camels have even stopped grumbling. The sun is burning my back and arms and legs, but I can't bear having any clothes on even though I know, this time, I'll blister for sure.

We jolt on for another hour. Or is it two?

My head is thumping. Salty sweat stings my eyes. My lips have cracked from the sun and from licking them so much. Now I can't even get any saliva in my mouth.

We've been careful with the water so there's plenty left. I get one of the bottles out and take another sip. Just before I pass the bottle to Walid, I see something ahead.

"A town! Thank God! Walid! Come on!" I kick Humphreda hard and she takes off. I drop the bottle and what's left in it spills. It doesn't matter. We've found an oasis.

"*La*, Ad-am!" I think he is being taunted by the magic of the sun and the desert.

It must be an oasis. I can see the whole town. The square white buildings, a mosque with tall minarets.

Then, it vanishes.

"Where did it go?"

All I can see now is an escarpment about four meters high and a few blocks of stone against the vertical, reddish surface.

Mirage.

I thought mirages were only meant to be of water. I can't believe I was fooled by a trick of the atmosphere and a few old stones. I could have sworn I saw buildings. This is the final straw. I feel the anger welling up inside me and then I lose it. What's the point of trying to stay calm? When my head feels as hot as this, I've got to let it all out somehow. I'm so mad I kick Humphreda as hard as I can. She's had enough of me, too, and does a sort of sideways swerve around nothing. I can't hold on.

"La!" Ad-am is falling. And that bad camel is running fast away. Too fast. With the camel, all our water has gone! But I cannot chase this camel. I must help Ad-am. He lies so still.

The sand beneath my feet is burning, but Adam's head is hotter still and his skin is dry.

He still breathes. Praise Allah! But he needs water or he will die. I am remembering Yasub, who ran away into the desert after Breath of Dog gave him a beating. When he came back after, in the afternoon, his head was hot and his skin too dry, but Breath of Dog said that he was bad so he did not deserve any water. Soon, Yasub was dead.

I run to the bottle Ad-am dropped on the ground, but all the water has spilled out and has vanished into the sand.

We must follow the tracks of the other camel and find her. But she might be far away, and, without water, Ad-am could die soon. Then, I am thinking and remembering one time what Old Goat did to a camel to make it give up water.

I will try this.

"Do not look at me so," I say to this camel, as I hold my camel stick tightly. "It will not be hurting." But this one knows I am not being truthful.

With difficulty I open her jaws. She is groaning and trying to bite. I jab the stick, hard and quickly, into her gullet. She chokes and coughs and sicks up water onto this shirt. Now I can wrap it around the head of Ad-am and make him cool.

I sort of come to and find that Walid has wrapped a damp shirt around my head.

I'm still burning all over. I need shade. I need water.

"We must find good water, for surely you are dying," I say to Ad-am. He is too red and hot and dry. "We will follow in the tracks of the bad camel and try to catch her. It is our only hope."

Walid drags me up onto his camel, in front of him. It's good he's holding me on because I feel really sick. Am I motion sick or have I got heatstroke? Maybe both. I just wish all the swaying would stop.

I shut my eyes to stop the blurriness.

"*Aiee!*"

Walid screeches and I open my eyes. We're on the crest of a dune and nestled in a valley below I can see a little oasis.

"It's only a mirage," I mutter. This one's even better than the last though because, although it's not as large, it's got a plantation of date palms. I shut my eyes. I don't want to be fooled again.

But Walid thinks it's real, and so does the camel. It snorts like it's happy.

We charge down the dune, swaying madly, and I open my eyes again. I wait for the dusty buildings to turn into stones. They don't. It's only when I feel the slight drop in temperature as we reach the shade of the date palms that I truly believe it's real.

I know for sure when I see Humphreda. She's got her nose stuck in a *falaj*, one of the water channels used to irrigate the date palms. Trust her!

As my eyes adjust to the shade after coming out

of the glare of the sun, I see men in purple-tinted *thobes,* the robes the Bedu wear. They're gathered around the camel, waiting for us.

None of them looks that friendly.

Then I see him—that black beard and the scowl.

It's Humphreda's owner.

CHAPTER TWENTY
SUNSET AT THE OASIS, DAY THREE

My skin feels like it's shrunk. It's too tight for my body and—I knew it—I'm starting to break out in blisters. These ropes that the Bedu have tied us up with feel as if they're scraping my skin off every time I move a muscle.

I don't know why they've tied us up. They've put us in this storage shed, which is made from mud bricks that are about half a meter deep. There's no way we can escape. There's a thick wooden door that looks like it's been made to withstand a charging tank, and no windows—only a tiny breeze hole, which has even got bars on it. It's so small, even skinny Walid wouldn't be able to get through. And, from the loud jabbering that's going on outside, we're being well guarded.

I roll over on the dirt floor to try and get more comfortable, but it feels like someone is pricking me with a thousand needles. It hurts so much I want to cry. But I'm not going to. I'm almost thankful for the pain because, while I'm concentrating on that, it stops me thinking about what's going to happen to us now.

I try to smile at Walid.

"We've got to stick together. Whatever happens."

"Now surely we will suffer the punishment of Allah for stealing," I tell Ad-am. "After *Mahgreb* they will judge us. I will pray to Allah to be merciful, but even if He is, I am sure the men will not be, for stealing camels is a terrible deed."

Through the breeze hole I see the sky redden as the sun sets, and sure enough, the next thing we hear is the wail of the call to sunset prayer.

As Walid kneels down, facing the red sky, and mutters his prayers, I say a few prayers myself. Surely these men will see that we weren't really trying to steal the camels. We had no choice. If only I could speak Arabic and explain it all properly.

I'm so busy trying to think up a plan, I don't realize the prayers have finished until the door swings open.

A shaft of light enters first, slanted like in one of

those pictures from the Bible when God is talking to someone. A sandaled foot with dirty toenails comes through the door, and a hand carrying a lantern.

I suddenly feel as if I've been magic-carpeted back about five hundred years.

The lantern carrier is the *Imam*. He's the local holy man. I can tell by the way his beard has been left to grow, like a wild bush sprouting off his chin, and he's got that I'm-one-step-closer-to-God-than-you look.

He starts going on at us. All the other men, led by Humphreda's owner, crowd into the small room. Our man still looks angry. He waves his hand in the air and speaks loudly.

Walidun. Jemaal. Inshala. These are the only words I can understand. Everyone is talking too quickly and loudly. But the *Imam* is loudest of all. He goes on and on and on, like he's lecturing us, just like our headmaster back at school. Then I hear Walid gasp.

I look over at him, and for somebody who should be brown he looks awfully white. I look over at the owner of the camels. I see he's grinning, showing sharp yellow teeth and making a chopping movement with his hand on his right wrist.

Suddenly, I'm not burning all over. I'm cold, and I feel my insides starting to turn to water.

They wouldn't.

Would they?

My brain feels numb, and the only words going through my head are "eye for an eye, tooth for a tooth."

I clench my fists hard, and close my eyes tightly to stop any tears leaking out.

Just then, the men in the doorway turn, as if someone else is coming. They all start talking at once, like they're explaining to someone new what's been going on. I hear the words *walid* and *fuloos*— "boy" and "money."

Suddenly, the whole atmosphere in the room changes. From anger to excitement. Next thing, the *Imam* holds up his hand and everyone shuts up.

He says something to the camel owner. It's a question. The man frowns and, after thinking for a while, he holds up four fingers. He begins to talk and wave his hands about. The others are nodding.

I think I know what's going on, but I don't want to get my hopes up. I look across at Walid to make sure. He's not frowning; he definitely looks happier.

I can't believe it, but it seems to be true. Someone is offering to pay for our camels—which should mean we'll be free. But why would someone out here, in the middle of nowhere, want to help us?

The crowd at the door makes way for someone.

Into the room comes . . .

"Breath of Dog!"

CHAPTER TWENTY-ONE
NIGHT AT THE OASIS, DAY THREE

It takes hours of haggling and endless cups of coffee, but finally the men come up with an agreed price and everyone seems happy.

Except us. What's going to happen now? I don't want to think about it.

"Ah, *walidun*—boys—I am being happy to be paying your debts and to be making you be free," Baggy Pants says in his broken English. He smiles and looks at both of us like he's Mr. Nice Guy as he pays out a wad of dirhams to the Bedu.

"Now I can be looking after and taking you to your good home." He comes over and pats me on the head.

I hate people patting me on the head. I'm not a dog.

Why are they paying for us? It cannot be for me—they must want Ad-am, for Breath of Dog is talking to him nicely in English. They will get good money for selling him to the *dalals*. I will not let them take my friend. I will not go quietly.

"I'd rather be dead or wandering forever in Hell on Earth."

"Yay, Walid!" I say, as he shouts and spits at Baggy Pants. The smile almost goes for a few seconds as Baggy Pants's eyes glitter, but he strokes his long, drooping moustache and looks around at the gathered men. He shrugs.

"*Walidun*," he says, in a way that makes the other men nod and frown, like they think we should be grateful to this man.

Ah, Allah! Now Breath of Dog will be shooting me for sure, but I am thinking of a plan . . .

Luckily I'm too busy thinking about how much pain I'm in to worry much about anything else. I wish Baggy Pants would loosen the ropes. At least that would ease some of the pain. I ache all over and my lips are blistered so it even hurts to talk, but more than anything else, the rope scraping my arms feels like someone is continually giving me a Chinese burn. But he doesn't untie us. I guess he doesn't want to take any chances on either of us escaping.

"Now to be taking you home," he says again, as he picks me up first and throws me over his shoulder. Then he grabs Walid and holds him under his arm. He's a big man—he can carry us both easily.

I clench my fists hard to stop myself yelling from the pain of having my raw skin scratched, as we make our way through the crowd of men and out of the building.

It's dark outside. I've no idea what the time is now. With my hands tied, I can't even look at my watch.

From my upside-down view, I see the Toyota truck. I notice it's got four brand-new tires.

Next thing, we're being shoved into the back and Old Orange Beard is looking over the seat at us and grinning. His scraggly beard is still colored with henna, and he looks like an old, toothless billy goat.

"*Bait*—home," he says in his high-pitched voice, and taps me on the head with his long camel stick. He starts to cackle.

I wish they really would take me home. I'm suddenly flooded with homesickness. I'd even be happy to see my sister. But now I know there's not much chance of me ever seeing my family again. Look what they did to Walid. This time I know we're done for.

Baggy Pants stuffs a rag into my mouth. It tastes like it's been used to clean an engine. He throws an old blanket over us that smells like sweaty armpits. Where will he take us now?

My mind starts to race with possibilities. Each worse than the one before. Will they just dump us somewhere in the desert? No, not likely after having shelled out all that money. They'll want some return.

Maybe we'll get sold on the slave market—we'll end up having a limb lopped off and we'll be put to work begging on the streets in India. Or, maybe I'll be forced to ride camels. I'm small for my age. They use small boys as camel jockeys.

Walid is wriggling and fidgeting under the blanket. I give him a sharp jab in his back with my elbow, but it doesn't stop him. My head feels as if it's going to explode, and the blanket is prickling me, hurting my sunburned back even more.

I need to keep my eyes tightly closed to hold back the tears, but it gives me something to do and helps me stop thinking.

We seem to drive for ages. I try to count the time so I can keep track of how far we've traveled, but my horrible thoughts and the pain of my burning skin keep distracting me.

I notice that the roads have become smoother now. We're not jolting around so much. We must be close to a town. Maybe Abudai.

A chink of light comes in through a hole in the blanket. I wriggle around until I can peer through it. I see buildings I recognize. We're on the southern side of Abudai.

Suddenly we pull up. I get the fright of my life because I see the face of a soldier looking through the window into the truck. We must be at a checkpoint. Wow! There still must be a war going on. But who's in charge now? The soldier has got a small moustache and is wearing a red beret. Is he a local or a Mafi? I can't tell. All their uniforms look the same.

The soldier asks Baggy Pants some questions. It's all in Arabic. Baggy Pants passes the soldier papers. The soldier asks more questions. Baggy Pants answers with a grunt and the soldier waves us on.

We travel through the outskirts of Abudai and I think about Tara waiting at the gate for us to come home. So close, but so far. I have to squeeze my eyes tight to stop the tears.

They must be going to sell us. Oh God, if the Mafi are in charge we'll probably be taken over there and end up in a carpet factory or worse.

"*Yameen, seedha, yassar.*" Old Orange Beard is giving directions. Being tied up, we roll this way and that as we swing around the corners. Walid is still wriggling like a worm.

At last! Praise Allah, it has been a long journey for it has given me time. Now to Ad-am.

"*Walhumdillah!*"

I roll over again as we go around yet another corner, and I hear Walid praising Allah. I can't exactly see anything to be thankful for.

"Ow!" I complain, as I feel the ropes being jerked hard against my wrists. Then, suddenly, the pain is gone. I wriggle my hands. I can move them. The rope isn't there. It takes me a second or so to work out what's happened.

No wonder Walid was fidgeting so much. He's managed to get the knife out of his pocket, open it up, and cut the ropes.

CHAPTER TWENTY-TWO
LATE EVENING IN ABUDAI, DAY THREE

What a kid! Walid just doesn't know how to give up.
Thank God.

I pull the rag out of my mouth. Now we've got a
chance of escaping. As soon as we stop, we can jump
out of the truck and run for it.

"*Bas*—enough," says Orange Beard. "This is being
it."

Baggy Pants grunts and slams the brakes on. We
jerk to a halt.

"Go!"

Walid and I leap up and, before the two men in
the front can even turn around, I've opened the car

door and I'm jumping out into the dark street with Walid right behind me.

"Allah! You crazy Ad-am. You have forgotten your bag." But as I grab the bag of Ad-am, Old Goat is seeing and he is holding fiercely to the straps.

"This time, Walid, you are being dead for sure," he is hissing, and his eyes are bulging with anger.

My throat is too parched to be spitting and my heart is thumping, yet never am I letting go. We cannot leave our food and water—and all that chocolate.

"May your heart be picked out by one thousand crows," I screech at Old Goat.

As I take off, with my feet hardly hitting the ground, two things register in my head. Walid is screaming like a stuck cat and the gate I'm running toward is the gate to our compound.

I can't believe it. They have brought me home.

But why? This can't be happening! It's got to be some trick. But it is my home. I can even hear Tara barking—going crazy like she does when she thinks somebody is near our house.

"Tara!" I yell, and next thing she jumps the high concrete fence around our house and is hurtling toward me, her tail going like crazy. She's whimpering and squealing the way she does when any of us gets home after being away for ages.

At first, I am thinking it is one wild dog attacking Ad-am and that he is in great danger, but I hear him call the name of Tara and I know this must be the one he loves too much.

"Kill the mad dog!" Old Goat is screeching to Breath of Dog. He will shoot her, just like Shirin.

"No! Ad-am!" I am screaming, screaming.

I hear Walid scream like he's being stabbed or something. I quickly turn to see what's happened. Oh, no! Walid is trying to get my bag from Old Orange Beard.

"Just leave it!" I yell at him, but of course, he doesn't understand me and he just holds on tighter.

Then Baggy Pants jumps out of the truck. He smacks Walid over the head with the end of his gun. Walid jerks backwards, but he still hangs on to the backpack. He's one tough nut, this kid.

"Let him go!" I scream at the men, and I feel so angry I don't even care that Baggy Pants is ten times bigger than me and has a gun.

I start to run back towards the truck—to help Walid. Tara's right behind me, barking.

But as I take the first step, I see Baggy Pants put his gun to his shoulder. He looks down the sights. But he's not pointing it at me. He's pointing it at Tara. And he won't miss at this range.

"No! Tara!"

There's nothing I can do to stop him.

Always killings. Too much killings. And Ad-am will cry and go crazy like after the death of the goat. I won't let them kill this dog the way they killed my Shirin.

Suddenly I see Walid let go of the backpack, leap up on Baggy Pants's back and pull at his arm. There's a cracking sound as the gun fires.

Tara yelps. She hits the ground, hard, and rolls over. It's only then that everything seems to speed up and all the action happens at once.

Tara takes off, yelping like mad, holding one leg at a funny angle. She streaks past two soldiers running out of our compound. One of them shouts something in Arabic.

"Halt!" I hear someone yell, in English this time. I stop, but Baggy Pants doesn't. He jumps back into the truck and, with a loud squeal of rubber, he and Old Orange Beard take off. Walid comes running towards me, yelling.

"Policemen! We must run fast away or they will be catching us and we will go to prison."

If nobody else is halting, then I'm not either. I have to find Tara and see if she's okay. She might be bleeding.

"Ad-am! Do not go that way for the policemen will catch you."

Suddenly something leaps onto my back. I know it's Walid. I can hear him screaming at me before I go head first into the road.

PART THREE
THE NADIR

CHAPTER TWENTY-THREE
MORNING AT THE AMERICAN MILITARY
BASE HOSPITAL, DAY FOUR

When I come to, the first thing I see is Walid's grin.
He's eating a chocolate ice cream. He's finally taken
the jocks off his head and he's wearing a baseball cap
instead. It's big and makes him look smaller, somehow, and younger than when he was wearing the
underduds.

"Where are we?"

At last! Now I know for sure Ad-am is alive, for, like
always, as soon as he awakens he begins to talk. But he
has been asleep for so long he doesn't know anything of
what has happened.

"The policemen have caught us and now we are in prison," I tell him. "But it is not as Old Goat is always saying. The prison is a good place—just like Paradise."

Walid tells me something in Arabic. I see now that he has a large white Band-Aid on his neck and iodine all over his arms and face where he has cuts and scratches. The bruises on his arms and legs from the car accident have turned blue, and he's got a black eye from where he hit his head. But he looks happy.

"Where are we?" I ask him again, even though I know he can't understand me.

"You're in the hospital—the American Military Base Hospital," a voice tells me in an American accent. I look up and I see, behind Walid, a tall man wearing a white coat and a crew cut hairstyle. "Do you know your name?"

I tell him.

"Okay, Adam," he says. "What day of the week is it today?"

I'm not too sure about that because it seems such a long time ago when there were normal things like days of the week. I can't even think what day it was when this whole nightmare started. I shrug and he frowns.

"What school do you go to?"

I tell him that and he seems pleased.

"Can you count my fingers?" He holds up three so I tell him that too.

"That's good, Adam." I don't understand why he's asking these dumb questions.

"Just tell me what happened," I say.

"You had an altercation with a road and the road won. And boy oh boy, you've got a beautiful black eye. Along with a very bad case of sunburn. But don't worry, you'll live. And I know what I'm talking about because I'm a doctor." He's speaking to me in that way adults do when they think they're being jokey with kids.

I put my hand to my head and feel an egg-shaped bump on my forehead.

"How did we get here?" It feels like ages since I heard proper English, so I should be happy, but the way he's carrying on is starting to irritate me. Whether he senses that or what, I don't know, but he becomes a bit more serious.

"You were both brought in last night by one of our soliders who was on patrol with the local military checking out the compounds, making sure there were no Unfriendlies lurking about. What were you two kids doing wandering around in a war zone anyway? Don't you know wars are a health hazard?"

"The war . . . what's happening?" I shake my head to jiggle my memory back into some sort of order, because at the moment, scraps of conversation, thoughts, and images are as messed up as a well-shuffled pack of cards.

"It's almost all over," the doctor tells me. "It's only taken three days, but it's been a pretty crazy three days." He shakes his head, then looks from Walid to me. "I don't know what you kids were up to—you and your friend here were in pretty bad shape—but I guess you'll have a story or two to tell your folks later. Now, someone will be in to see you both soon and find out all your details. We don't even know your pal's name yet, because no one here speaks Arabic. We've been waiting for you to wake up and tell us the full story."

"But I haven't got time to tell you everything," I tell him. "I've got to get out of here and find Tara." I try to get out of bed, but the doctor holds me down.

"Whoa there, sonny," he says. "You've had a concussion. You can't be out leaping around the place looking for people."

"But Tara was hurt and she could be bleeding to death."

"Who's Tara? What happened?" Suddenly the doctor's joking manner has gone. I'm pleased.

"She's my dog and Baggy Pants shot her. Or at least he tried to shoot her, but Walid pulled his arm down and he only shot her in the leg."

Then I remember it was Walid who jumped me. I look at him. He's got chocolate ice cream all around his mouth.

"You idiot," I say, but in a friendly way. I can't stay mad at him. He saved me when I was ready to give up. And he tried to make sure Tara wasn't shot.

"Oh, for a minute I thought you were talking about your sister or a friend." The doctor sounds relieved. "The dog will be alright."

"But I've got to find her. I've gone through so much to rescue her. I've got to get out of here. She was shot in the leg and she'll be scared." The doctor mustn't have understood what I said before.

But he did. He just didn't care.

"Look, young man, let's get this straight." His jokey tone is completely gone. "You are staying right here. It's only a dog and we have people—soldiers and civilians—to worry about. Besides, even if you hadn't had a concussion we wouldn't let you out of here. You're both much too young to sign yourselves out. You'll have to wait until your parents or some other relation or guardian comes to pick you up."

"That could be days," I say, but he isn't listening.

"Now, here's the liaison officer. If you give all your details to him, he'll help find out where your parents are. They must be worried sick."

The liaison officer looks about Sarah's age. He isn't interested in hearing our story, either. All he wants are the basic facts. Name, address, nationality. He writes everything down on a big form.

"Right," he says. "That should be enough detail to find your parents. Now, what about your friend?" He turns to Walid. "Do you speak English?"

Walid grins and nods.

"Choc-o-late!"

"That's the only word he knows," I tell the liaison officer, who doesn't see the funny side.

"They didn't tell me he couldn't speak English. They should have sent an interpreter with me. Do you speak Arabic?"

I shake my head. "Not really."

The liaison officer looks confused.

"He is with you, isn't he? They said you came in together."

"Yeah," I reply. "We came in together."

"Do you know his name and where he's from then?"

"His name's Walid . . ." I start to say, and then I realize I really don't know anything at all about him. I know he can spit like a champion and ride a camel really well, and that he can slit a goat's throat and that he doesn't give up even when everything looks hopeless, but I don't have a clue what his real name is or where he's from. I don't even know what his relationship is with Baggy Pants and Old Orange Beard.

I hesitate.

"He is your friend, isn't he?" The liaison officer asks, sounding impatient. "Or is he your maid's son or something?"

"No," I say. "He's not Chandra's son. He . . . he's . . ."
How can I tell this person that Walid is better than any
mate I've ever had? If I'd been stuck in the desert with
Jason or Nigel or Jean-Marie or any of the others we'd
have all ended up dead. But it's not just that he saved
my life. Walid's got guts. And he's funny and smart. I
guess it doesn't matter that I don't know his real name
or where he lives.

The liaison officer is still looking at me like I
should have all the answers.

"Walid's my friend, but I . . . I . . ." I just don't feel
like trying to explain it all to this officer so I take the
easy way out. "I'm feeling tired now."

The doctor, who is still there, immediately steps in.

"He's had a concussion. I think it's best if you
leave the questions for later. As long as you've got
enough to find at least one of their parents—this one
needs to rest."

"Okay." The young officer stands up. "I guess I'll
bring an interpreter back when I can and we'll get
this other kid's details then. In the meantime, I'll get
in touch with the Australian Embassy and pass on
this information. Your mom and pop'll be pleased to
know you're safe."

I nod, but don't speak. What's the point?

"I have to go, too," says the doctor, "but I'll make
sure you both get your medication—that is, chocolate
ice cream, of course." And he winks at me.

CHAPTER TWENTY-FOUR
MORNING AT THE AMERICAN MILITARY BASE HOSPITAL, DAY SEVEN

"Somehow we've got to get out of here," I say to Walid. But I know we can't escape this time. "They've told me we have to stay here until someone arrives to claim us. It's like we're lost property or something."

But it'll be days before Mum and Dad get here. When they found out where I was through the embassy, they rang me. Even though I really wanted to speak to them, I was a bit scared because I thought they'd tell me off. They did. But, luckily, they didn't have a lot of time to talk because I was on a hospital phone.

"We'll try to get on a plane as soon as the airport reopens for civilian flights," Mum told me after she calmed down. "But at the moment no one but essential personnel and, of course, journalists, are allowed back. Now, you stay put until we get there. No more brilliant ideas, please."

"We're as much in prison in this hospital as we were in the village," I say to Walid. "They've even locked the door to make sure we don't run away. Can you believe it? How could we get this close, and yet still be as far away as we were when we were in the mountains. I could kick something."

And I do, because if I try to keep it all in, the top of my head is going to blow off with frustration.

Walid holds out another ice cream to me. He hasn't stopped eating them since I woke up. I suppose that's all there is to do. And it is good ice cream—thick and creamy. Maybe it will even help to cool me down. My skin is still sore from the blisters.

Then the door of our room opens and in walks . . .

A princess! Never have I seen such a *jameelatun*—such a beauty. She has hair like the shining sun and eyes more blue than the sky.

It's my sister. I can hardly believe it. "Sarah?" I ask, because, although I know it's her, she looks different. No kidding, she's troweled the makeup onto her face and she's wearing a fancy suit. It makes her look so old—at least twenty-two or something.

"What are you doing here?"

She waves some papers at me.

"I'm here to get you out and take you home," she says. "I've signed everything and they're letting you and your friend here go into my care."

"But where's Mum and Dad?" I ask.

"I guess they're probably on their way back here by now," says Sarah airily.

I shake my head because I still can't quite grasp what's going on.

"How did you get here?"

"On an airplane, of course," says my smart-aleck sister.

"Yeah, alright," I say, guessing that she's either used the return ticket Mum makes us keep or even bought one with the credit card Mum lets her have for emergencies. "But you know what I mean. How come you're here? Mum said they're not letting any-one back into the country yet."

"When I heard that you'd done your usual dumb thing of running away, I figured you might need some help so I skipped school myself. I knew the Australian authorities would never let me go if I said I was trying to get here so I dressed up a bit, put lots of makeup on and bought a ticket to Singapore. It was easy from there. They don't care where you go as long as you have a ticket, which I did thanks to Mum, and I was able to get on board one of the first flights back here, not long after the airport was reopened. I didn't think I'd find you safe in hospital."

"But how did you get priority?" I ask. "There must have been heaps of people trying to come back in."

"Well, they did think I was a journalist." She flashes an impressive-looking press badge at me.

"Hey! That's the badge Dad made for you on the computer, for that Compound News Network project of yours."

"Well, as you can see, I'm a reporter for CNN, or at least that's what the people at the embassy who signed my papers believe."

I shake my head. Only my big sister would have the brains to think up a plan like that and then the nerve to pull it off. She's pretty cool.

"Do Mum and Dad know you're here?" I ask, but I figure I know the answer.

"I guess they do by now," says Sarah. "And I guess they're on their way home as we speak so we could both be in a bit of trouble . . ."

This is the old Sarah. I grin because it's fantastic to see her again.

"By the way, I have to admit it wasn't my idea to offer those characters who had your mobile a reward for bringing you home. It was Barby's cunning plan. That must be where I get my brilliance from, though."

I look blankly at her. "A reward?"

"Didn't Mum tell you? Barby rang your mobile and she got this crazy old guy who spoke a bit of English. He said he might know where to find you, so she got in touch with a local television network and they put up a reward for your rescue."

So that was it. That was why Baggy Pants and Old Orange Beard took me home. They'd been hoping to make some money out of me.

"How much of a reward was being offered?" I'm so curious.

"Ten thousand dollars," Sarah tells me. "Mum's even been on television appealing for help."

"Wow! I'm impressed. Before Mum left she was so mad at me I would have thought she'd have paid that much to get rid of me."

"I guess she changed her mind," says Sarah, and for a second, there's a slightly gooey look on her face like she's about to cry, but that quickly changes. "God knows why. And anyway, what happened to the old guy? Did he bring you here? How did he find you?"

"It's a bit of a long story," I say. "Can we just get out of here and go home and see if Tara's okay?"

"I've got a taxi waiting outside. Now you'd better introduce me to your friend here, seeing as I'm rescuing him as well."

Walid is staring at Sarah like he's never seen a western girl before.

"His name is Walid," I say. "But he doesn't speak English. He only speaks Arabic."

"*Alaykum as-salaam,*" she says to Walid, which even I understand because it means "peace be upon you" and it's the way to say hello in Arabic.

"Alaykum as-salaam. Old Goat told me all foreign girls are ugly and bad, but you have the beauty of a princess."

Sarah giggles like she's a kid, then she starts to jabber away to Walid, who jabbers back. I didn't know she could speak Arabic so well. She really is amazing.

"That's terrible," she says, and then she turns to me with that fierce look on her face she gets when she's on the warpath about something. "Did you know he was sold to traders when he was seven years old? His family couldn't afford to keep him. He's been living in a camp just outside the city. He's been a camel jockey!"

"Um . . . no," I have to admit.

"My God, what sort of life has he had to live?" I know she doesn't expect an answer this time. And she doesn't give me a chance anyway, but it explains a few things—like why Walid could ride a camel like an expert.

"And," she goes on, "those dreadful men he was sold to tied him up and left him in the mountains as a punishment because they said he was bad. At least he's got a mother here somewhere working as a maid. Maybe Mum and Dad will be able to track her down through the Bangladeshi Embassy."

I can hardly believe it. In about three minutes, Sarah has found out more about Walid than I knew after being with him for about a week.

"Right," says Sarah. "First things first, though. We need to get home and make sure Tara is okay."

The streets of Abudai are still fairly deserted, which isn't much different from every other summer when lots of people get out of here anyway, but today the only people to be seen are soldiers. And there are still the marks of the war everyone's now calling the Three Day War—not very imaginative. The Centra Tower is not shining like it usually does. It's black, and the windows around the top ten or so stories are broken. But it's still standing. Other buildings have got bullet holes in them, and the taxi has to swerve around big craters in the road where bombs have landed.

"How come you didn't run away when the war was on?" Sarah asks our taxi driver after she finds out he comes from Baluchistan, where he has a wife and ten children at home and his latest newborn is a boy.

"Where to go?" the taxi driver shrugs. "My sponsor is keeping my passport and he is running fast away. Anyway, what matter is it to me who is winning or losing one war? Always taxis is being needed and in times such as this the fares are being greater so it is being good business."

True to his word, he charges us three times too much for the ride from the hospital to our compound. Sarah doesn't even argue.

I hardly wait for the taxi to pull up before I jump out and run towards the big, heavy wooden gates.

"Wait for us," Sarah calls out as she and Walid follow, but I've already waited too long to find out if Tara is okay.

I drag back one of the gates. Why isn't Tara barking? She must have heard the taxi. Usually she'd be going crazy by now.

I go cold all over.

"Tara! Tara!" I yell, as I race through the gates. Then I see our door is open. That's weird. Briefly I wonder if the soldiers are checking it out for Unfriendlies again. I don't care, I have to find Tara. I have to find out if she's dead or alive.

As I get to the step, I hear a whimper and the clickety clack of her nails on the tiles inside the house.

Tara skids out through the door and squeals when she sees us. She's limping a fair bit and is fairly skinny, but she's okay.

"Hey, girl," I say, as I rub her ears and lean down to hug her, breathing in her warm, buttery-toast smell. "We're home now."

"Not for long. You're both going to be on the first plane out of here and there'll be no arguments." It's Dad. He's still in his uniform, which is a bit crumpled, and it doesn't look as if he's shaved for about three days. The door was open so he must have just arrived. I can see he's trying to look cross, but it doesn't work.

"Dad!" I yell and rush over to him. He grabs me and Sarah and gives us both a big hug that almost smothers me, but I don't care.

It's Tara who reminds me that Walid has just been standing there, on his own, watching us. She goes over and sniffs at him in a friendly way. I can see by the way he's standing so still and by the look in his eyes that he's scared, but, typical Walid, he's not going to let anyone know.

"She likes you," I say to him. "And she's not going to hurt someone who's saved her life."

"What's this about saving your life?" asks Dad. "And who is that?"

"It's a long story," I tell him, as I go over and save Walid from Tara. "But if it weren't for Walid . . ." I gulp. With everyone being all emotional, I find it hard to hold back the tears when I think about the last seven days and how close Baggy Pants came to shooting Tara. If it weren't for Walid . . .

CHAPTER TWENTY-FIVE
AFTERNOON IN ADUBAI, WEEK TWO

Dad didn't make us go back out on the first plane, after all. He said we could wait until Mum came back. Then when Mum came back, crying bucket-loads of tears in between blasting us, we got another reprieve. Sarah, of course, was the one to work out the way to stay a bit longer.

"We can't go," she said, "not while Walid is here on his own. Adam's his only friend and I can inter-pret for him."

Mum said we could stay a week.

After lunch on our last day in Abudai, Sarah men-tions the reward. I'd almost forgotten about the ten thousand dollars.

"I hope those awful men aren't going to get that money even though they did bring Adam back."

"Never!" My mum suddenly sounds fierce. "They tried to kill the boys! And it's utterly shocking the way they buy little children from those greedy traders and make them ride camels in those dreadful races. Children as young as three on top of a camel! Can you imagine? All for the entertainment of rich sheikhs! They could give away the money they spend on those racing camels and keep half of Bangladesh in food for years."

My mum's on her soapbox and well away. I guess that's where Sarah gets it from.

"I can't even imagine what this poor boy's life must have been like," she begins.

Dad just sighs and looks at his watch for about the hundredth time and mutters about somebody being late.

Walid and I have had conversations with Sarah interpreting, but there's still so much I don't understand about his life.

"But how could his mother give him away like that?" I want to know. It seems so cruel. My mum might get a bit annoyed with me, but she would never sell me into that sort of life.

Of course, Sarah has another opinion and isn't slow in coming forward with it.

"If Mum had had the choice of us both starving to death in Bangladesh or giving us what she believed would be a chance to be educated and make some money, I think she would have done exactly the same thing."

Maybe. I don't really want to think about it. But with a life like Walid's had it's not surprising that he's such a tough nut.

Now that my mum's spent hours scrubbing him, he looks different from the Walid I first met. He didn't like being cleaned up much, but there's no arguing with my mum when it comes to cleanliness. She even got him to take off the filthy *dishdash* so she could wash it. But the one thing you can't take away from him, though, is that grin.

Such a wonderful palace Ad-am lives in. But one thing I do not understand is why, with so much eating, Ad-am is not big and tall. Maybe it is because of sleeping in one soft bed and too much washing in water.

I grin back.

"Things are going to be different now," says Dad. "I've got a bit of a surprise for you."

Just then the doorbell rings.

"I'll get it." Mum jumps up and runs to the door. I've never seen her act like this before.

On the step are two Arabic men wearing the traditional white *dishdash* and flowing headdress. With them is a small, dark-skinned Indian-looking man with a moustache. He's wearing a suit and looks important. One of the Arabic men looks familiar, and then I realize who it is.

So does Mum.

"Your Excellency . . ." For once, she's lost for words. I glance out through the doorway and I can see, standing at the gate, half a dozen Arabic and American soldiers. All of them are armed. It's not surprising. On our doorstep is Sheikh Abdulla, the Prime Minister of Abudai.

"*As-salaam alaykum*—the peace of Allah upon you," says Sheikh Abdulla.

"*Alaykum as-salaam,*" Mum replies automatically. It's about the only Arabic she knows. She puts out her hand.

"I'm Jannette McCourt," she says, but Sheikh Abdulla only nods his head politely.

Mum looks down at her hand, and then looks really flustered.

But I know she's not worried that he's treating her like she's beneath him. Mum's always going on about how polite Arabic men are and that the average western man could learn a lot from the way they treat women. Even though he's refusing to take her hand, the sheikh is actually treating her with respect. Mum's flustered because she forgot that in Arabic culture it's discourteous to touch a woman, even to shake her hand.

The sheikh turns to my dad and speaks in perfect English. "This, as you must know, is his Excellency, the Ambassador of the Bangladeshi Embassy, Mr. Chaudry."

The important-looking Indian man bows politely. "And this is Mohammed Al Shamsi."

"Ah!" my dad says, as if he's heard the name before. "But we weren't expecting such a delegation."

"It is important after such an incident as we have experienced to show the people that all is well. Also, when I was told of this story I wished to meet these two brave young boys. And there are one or two delicate matters . . ."

As he says this, he steps aside, and it's only then I see that behind him is a small lady with a long dark plait that reaches most of the way down her back. She's wearing a sari and has worried-looking eyes.

"Mama! It's my mama!"
"Emir! My little prince!"

The small woman squeezes between the men,

dashes towards Walid and hugs him tightly as if she's never going to let him go.

"Don't cry, Mama. I am happy. Look! I am also having many dirhams. Now I can care for you just like Babu said."

Walid's mum is crying. Mum and Sarah are, too. I almost am.

Dad invites the Sheikh of Abudai, the Bangladeshi Ambassador, and Mr. Al Shamsi in, as if he's used to doing this every day of his life. Mum pulls herself together then, and offers them all coffee.

"Mr. Chaudry has told me the whole story of these remarkable two boys." Here he looks in my direction and I can't help it—I go red. Even Walid seems stunned.

"But I wanted to hear the facts from the boys themselves. Adam and Emir, please can you tell us your story?"

So I tell my side in English and Walid tells his in Arabic. When we finish, the Sheikh looks thoughtful. "It seems," he says, "that if two such boys from different cultures can learn to live together and survive such a perilous journey, then there is something here for us adults." He grasps my dad by the shoulder and kisses him on both cheeks and, in true Arabic style, goes for the third kiss on the cheek.

I can't believe it, but my dad lets him, and he doesn't even seem embarrassed. In fact, he seems pleased.

"Yes, we could learn something from them both, that's for sure," he says. "And I have to say I am most impressed with the efficiency of your embassy officials, Mr. Chaudry. You've moved so quickly to find the boy's mother. Much more quickly than I would have expected under the circumstances, with the war just over."

"It was no major difficulty," says Mr. Chaudry, in a clipped English accent, as he strokes his small moustache. "We have a register of all the maids legally working here and, happily, this boy's mother had all the correct paperwork."

"Thank you, your Excellencies, for everything," Mum says, covering the lot of them in one address.

"It is our very great pleasure, Madam." Mr. Chaudry bows to Mum. "We in the Bangladeshi Embassy do our best in these tragic situations, but what can we do? Ours is a poor country . . ."

"And we have made laws to stop the terrible practice of buying and selling children to be used as camel jockeys," says Sheikh Abdulla. "The teachings of Islam do not condone this behavior, but many years of tradition are hard to break."

"We've got no right to be up on our high horse anyway." Sarah suddenly butts in. "It was only a hundred or so years ago that we were sending children up chimneys and down coal mines."

Trust Sarah to put in her bit. I have to grin as the men look slightly startled, but they're all too polite to acknowledge that there's an unmarried female in the room so they carry on as if she hadn't said a word.

"Kalyani has been working for us for four years now, but she never gave any hint that she had a son," says Mr. Al Shamsi.

The Ambassador nods. "It is the way of the *dalals*. They tell the mothers of these children never to speak of it if they want to see their sons again. The women feel they have no choice but to remain silent."

"So cruel," murmurs Mum. "How can human beings treat each other so badly?"

"We have a term in Arabic," says the sheikh. "It is *nadir*—the lowest point. This is, I believe, the nadir of human behavior."

I'm hardly listening any more. Ever since I saw Walid giving his mum those grubby old dirhams he's been hanging on to all this time, my brain has been ticking away in the background and then, at last, it all clicks.

"Hey!"

"Sounds like Mr. Smartypants has had one of his mind-bustingly brilliant brain waves again." Sarah's right back into her sarcastic mode.

"Well, it just so happens that I think this might

be one of the best," I say, then I ignore her and look at Mum and Dad. Even though the Ambassador of Bangladesh and the Sheikh of Abudai are looking over my shoulder, I've got to have my say.

"It's about that money—the reward. . . . You know, I think I know what to do with it."

Nobody says anything, so I take a deep breath and start to speak more quickly.

"I've probably made it sound like I was a bit of a hero on this adventure." I hear my sister snort, but I don't let it interrupt what I want to say. "The truth is, I'd never have got back here without Walid—I mean, Emir." Boy, it was going to be hard getting used to Walid's real name. I decide to stick with "Walid" for now. "I mean, we both had to stick together to get here. Sure I did have one or two good ideas, but, like, when I was ready to give up, he just wouldn't. And he actually saved my life a couple of times. I think if anyone's going to get a reward for rescuing me, then it should be Walid. Then he and his mum could go back to Bangladesh. With all that money they could live like . . . like sheikhs." I finish really fast because they're all staring at me. Even Walid and his mum, who don't understand a word I'm saying, are looking at me.

"Why didn't I think of that?" my dad says, as he winks at my mum who's snuffling again.

"Not a bad idea, little brother," my sister concedes. "But I'd really like to know how you two were able to communicate, so you could work out what to do. Walid doesn't speak a word of English and your Arabic is, it has to be said, hopeless, so how on Earth did you know what the other meant?"

Trust Sarah to ask a question like that, but I'm sort of pleased she asked because the atmosphere was about to get seriously sloppy. Again.

"Ask Walid," I say to her. So she does. Walid and I look at each other and shrug. Then, we jump up and we slam our hands together in a perfect high-five.

NOTE FROM THE AUTHOR

Because I'd always wanted to be a writer, I decided that when I left school I needed to go out into the world and collect experiences, so that when I had enough I could write about them.

I traveled around Australia and then around the world. The experiences I collected were many and varied; such as learning how to cook when I worked with shearers in the outback; learning how to fly when my husband and I ferried airplanes across to Canada and back; learning to teach when I taught English as a foreign language to Arab girls. Along the way I learnt about life.

I got my chance to write while living in Dubai

when I started working for a children's magazine. All my different experiences became useful. I had six columns to write—covering astronomy, astrology, science and technology, and gardening, as well as a weekly bedtime story and an advice column. There I also met an interesting old lady from Iran and helped her write her autobiography, which was later published.

My time in Dubai taught me more than how to write, though. I learnt that when people from different cultures meet, they often don't trust or respect each other, and there can be many misunderstandings that can even lead to war. But after having lived and made friends with people from other nationalities, I know that no culture is better than another; we just do things differently.

I wrote the first draft of *Camel Rider* while living in Dubai. We left there in March 2001 and we now live in magical "Rowan House," which overlooks the Sunshine Coast of Queensland and where I run a writers' retreat and guesthouse.